The SUV careened wildly down the road.

He tapped the brakes. The vehicle veered toward a drop-off that descended into a canyon. Pulling the steering wheel in the other direction, Josh stepped on the brakes with everything he had.

He managed to correct their course but the mountain road's sharp descent had them picking up even more speed.

"Josh?" Kylie's voice held a question.

"Hold on."

The narrow road was flanked by a sheer cliff on one side and the canyon on the other. Neither looked promising.

He pulled the emergency brake, but it barely put a beat in the SUV's momentum. He jerked on the wheel as his vehicle veered to the edge of the road again and did his best to muscle it away from the steep cliff.

But they were going over. The SUV was toppling into the steep canyon...

Jane M. Choate dreamed of writing from the time she was a small child when she entertained friends with outlandish stories complete with happily-ever-after endings. Writing for Love Inspired Suspense is a dream come true. Jane is the proud mother of five children, grandmother to ten grandchildren and staff to one cat who believes she is of royal descent.

Books by Jane M. Choate

Love Inspired Suspense

Keeping Watch
The Littlest Witness
Shattered Secrets
High-Risk Investigation
Inherited Threat
Stolen Child
Secrets from the Past
Lethal Corruption
Rocky Mountain Vendetta
Christmas Witness Survival
Rocky Mountain Survival

Visit the Author Profile page at LoveInspired.com.

Rocky Mountain Survival

JANE M. CHOATE

LOVE INSPIRED SUSPENSE
INSPIRATIONAL ROMANCE

LOVE INSPIRED®SUSPENSE
INSPIRATIONAL ROMANCE

ISBN-13: 978-1-335-59945-2

Rocky Mountain Survival

Copyright © 2024 by Jane M. Choate

PLEASE RECYCLE — THIS PRODUCT IS RECYCLABLE

Recycling programs
for this product may
not exist in your area.

For questions and comments about the quality of this book, please contact us
at CustomerService@Harlequin.com.

® is a trademark of Harlequin Enterprises ULC.

Love Inspired
22 Adelaide St. West, 41st Floor
Toronto, Ontario M5H 4E3, Canada
www.LoveInspired.com

Printed in U.S.A.

And this is the confidence that we have in him, that, if we ask any thing according to his will, he heareth us.
—*1 John* 5:14

Those who have read my other books know how I deeply admire the men and women of the United States Special Forces. They make it possible for us to sleep safely in our beds at night while they fight America's enemies. SEALs, Delta, Rangers, Marine Force Recon and others, this book is for you.

ONE

Cold.

Kylie Robertson had never minded the cold. Had, in fact, always enjoyed the bite of a Colorado winter. Until a year ago. Until…

Her hands ached. The cold aggravated the pain. That was to be expected. She didn't need to remove her gloves to see the scars that crisscrossed her palms like twisted barbed wire.

With one more violent shiver, more from the memory of how she'd gotten those scars than from the cold itself, Kylie let herself inside her condo.

She'd returned from the event early, realizing she'd forgotten to bring a different camera lens for the photos she wanted to take for her next story, those of a children's chorus singing at the birthday party of a 101-year-old veteran.

She turned the heat up and waited for warmth to fill the small space. The doll-sized condo had been all she could afford, but that would change—she hoped—when she sold her next series of photographs, especially those she'd taken today. She had high expectations for them, capturing expressions of those attending a speech concerning shootings in shopping malls and grocery stores, schools and churches.

Violence in the nation had grown to alarming proportions. By showing the pain and the grief, the bewilderment and the anger on the faces of the hundreds of individuals who had attended, she hoped to raise both awareness and outrage of what was happening.

She moved through her condo. Even the heavy coat she wore didn't completely ward off the cold. She'd turned down the heat before she left, trying to save on the gas bill that seemed to go up exponentially every month.

A highly charged mix of cheap aftershave and adrenaline-infused sweat alerted her that someone was in the condo with her. In the next instant, a thick arm clamped around her neck, threatening to cut off her air supply.

Panting, she fought against the attacker. She thrust her elbows up and back. He grunted as she connected with the soft tissue of his throat, but it wasn't enough to make him release her.

Her brain struggled to take in information and process it as her air supply diminished with every passing second. A few more seconds and she would pass out. Another couple of minutes would equal death.

She had survived six months in a prison camp run by a commandant so inhumane that even the guards flinched at what they were ordered to do. No way was she going to let some local goon snuff out her life now.

She needed to stay alive. She jabbed back at him again.

"Where is it?"

"Where's what?" she asked in a hoarse voice.

Her attacker loosened his hold on her enough that she could breathe. She let the oh-so-sweet air in and found she could think again.

She'd bide her time and strike when he least expected.

"The SD card."

Her SD card. It contained only the pictures she'd taken today of the crowd gathered to hear the governor's speech, and though she felt she'd captured some good images, there was nothing that warranted a threat to her life. "Why?"

"That don't concern you. Just give me the card, and you get to live."

"Big of you," she muttered.

In retaliation, he tightened the arm around her neck once more. "Do you want to play rough? 'Cause I'm good at that. I'm *really* good at it."

"No." She gasped out the single syllable in a desperate bid to suck in air.

"Okay." He eased the pressure on her windpipe. "Hand over the card and forget you ever took those pictures."

What made those pictures so important? "I think there's been some kind of mistake."

"Yeah. And the mistake is yours."

He didn't sound like the kind of man she could reason with, but it wouldn't hurt to try.

"I don't know—"

His grip on her tightened. "Hand it over."

"I'm trying to tell you that I don't know what you're talking about." The words came out in a rush. She strangled out a gasp that nearly caused her to choke.

"The SD card with the pictures you took today. I want it." Her attacker's voice thrummed with menace, and she shivered. It wasn't just fright; it was losing control. She had no idea what she was mixed up in and didn't like being in the dark. If he was going to kill her, she at least wanted to know *why*.

When she got her voice back, she asked, "What do you want with it?"

"My orders are to get that card. If you want to live long enough to take your next breath, you'll hand it over."

She believed him. She'd encountered bullies in school, in the workplace and then again in the hot spots of the world where despots and tyrants exerted their will on helpless people—and recognized the same swagger and meanness in her attacker. She wouldn't allow this one, with his bad breath and bossy attitude, to intimidate her.

She inhaled sharply. Not so much because she needed air, but because she was stalling for time. Time to decide what to do.

Despite that resolve, tremors invaded her body, making her all too aware of the weakness that had been her constant companion since she'd returned to the States.

She tried for meek to disguise her growing fury. "Please. You're scaring me." She didn't have to fake sincerity as that was the truth.

He leaned closer. "I'll do a lot more than that."

"They're just pictures of the crowd waiting to hear the governor speak." Though she doubted she'd convinced him, that was the truth. She had wanted the honest reactions of people who had gathered to hear the governor talk about shootings in the community.

"Quit lying."

"I'm not—" She wasn't given the opportunity to complete the sentence.

Her vision grayed; her skin grew clammy. Worse, her brain grew fuzzy. She was once more on the verge of passing out when he let up. Greedily, she sucked in what air she could.

"Like that?" he asked. "There's more where that came from. In fact, I can keep it up all day."

"Why?" She barely croaked out the word in a voice that sounded as raw as her throat felt. She should just hand over the card and hope he let her live, but something in her refused to obey the sensible advice. Could she be making someone captured in the pictures a target if she gave in to the man's demands?

"You don't need to know why. You just need to do it."

He tightened his hold again. Lack of oxygen shut down brain function. She felt it happening and was powerless to stop it. With the last remnants of her energy, she flailed her arms, but it did no good. Where were her carefully earned self-defense skills when she needed them?

"You act like you have a choice about this," the man taunted. "You don't. If you want to keep on breathing for another minute, you'll do as I say."

"You'll kill me anyway," she managed to get out.

"But there's dying, and then there's dying. Your choice."

The total lack of emotion in his voice frightened her far more than if he'd screamed at her.

"Okay. It's in my purse. Let me catch my breath, and I'll get it for you."

In truth, the card was in her pocket, but she wasn't about to tell him that. She'd put it there when her hands had been full as she'd switched out one camera for the other.

"No tricks," he warned.

"No tricks."

While she was talking, Kylie edged her right foot backward. She needed leverage if she was to make her move, one she'd learned in her Krav Maga classes. The instructor had drilled into her students to use whatever means they could to protect themselves. She'd have one opportunity to save herself and only one. She had to make it count.

When she still had made no attempt to retrieve the card, he snapped, "I'll get it myself."

She pointed to the kitchen table where her purse sat.

When he turned his back, she shifted her weight to her left leg and got ready.

He grabbed the purse, dumped the contents on the table. "There's no card here."

"I'm sure I put it in there." She worked to make herself sound confused, as though the situation had traumatized her.

If he only knew the truth, that she had already been broken both physically and emotionally, he might have pushed her harder. As it was, she was doing her best to hold it together and come up with a plan to come out of this alive.

He'd kill her once he had what he wanted. She saw it in the cold intent in his eyes, heard it in the dispassionate tone of his voice.

This was a job for him. No, *she* was a job for him. No more. No less.

He turned back to her. "You're asking for it, lady. Give me the card, and we'll end this."

"You'll let me go?" she asked with what she hoped was a convincing whimper.

"Yeah. I'll let you go. Why not?" The words were said on a sneer that made no attempt to be anything than what it was.

"You're not lying, are you?" She was stalling for time, going through the sequence of moves she needed to make.

"Lady, just shut up and give me what I came for."

"Here it is." She pivoted on her foot, then raised her knee and hit him squarely between his legs. The resounding thump felt good.

He shrieked like a wild animal that had gotten his leg caught in a trap. He dropped to the floor, screaming at her. The look in his eyes was one of pure agony. Beneath that, though, was the promise of retribution.

But she didn't waste time gloating. Instead, she grabbed her laptop.

He seized hold of her coat as she passed, but she didn't let that stop her and yanked herself free.

"You'll pay," he croaked out, still clearly unable to get up. "You'll pay for this."

The frigid morning air bit into her, all teeth and claws. Fortunately, she hadn't removed her coat as she had just walked in the door when her attacker grabbed her. Still, the cold was enough to cause her to gasp.

The fight-or-flight instinct kicked in. She had already fought. Now it was time for flight. She had one choice.

Run.

Even with her training, she knew she was no match for the man who had broken into her home. She'd gotten the better of him earlier because she'd taken him by surprise. He wouldn't be fooled again. Pain and probably a good dose of humiliation would make him want payback.

Her car was in the garage, which meant she'd have to go through the condo again to get to it, so that was a no-go. He'd be anticipating that.

Think.

Her cell was in her pocket. She pulled it out and punched in 911 and spat out the information.

"Can you get somewhere safe?" the operator asked. "I'll dispatch a unit to you, but it will take them five minutes to reach you. The storm has us spread pretty thin."

A block away was a local grocery store. If she could reach that, she could wait for the police to arrive. She gave the location of the supermarket.

And ran.

Snow-packed sidewalks from an unseasonal early storm made the going treacherous, but she couldn't slow down. A cold blast of wind whipped her exposed face. She heard the pounding of footsteps behind her but couldn't afford the seconds it would take to look back. Instead, she gave an extra burst of energy, increasing the distance between her and her pursuer. He wasn't as fast as she might have suspected; no doubt his injury had slowed him down.

She hadn't stopped him, no, but she'd given him something to think about.

Only a few yards more.

When she reached the store, she pushed open the door. The people there gave her odd looks with her wild eyes and windblown hair, but she didn't care and ducked behind a counter. The clerk must have sensed her desperation because he didn't say anything.

She decided her hiding place was too obvious and hid behind a large cart filled with items to be stocked. Her heart was beating so rapidly she feared she was having a cardiac arrest as she wondered whether the cops would show up before her attacker. Had he followed her into the store or had she lost him?

A couple minutes later, the police arrived, and she took her first easy breath since she'd felt her attacker's arm at her throat.

Two officers questioned her at length.

"You say you don't know why he wanted your card?" the patrolman asked for what seemed the fiftieth time.

"No." Her throat hurt, and she could barely get out the word.

"Do you have anywhere you can stay until we find out what's going on?" he asked.

"I don't know." That was the truth. Upon her return to the States six months ago, she'd rebuffed attempts from friends to connect with her. Eventually, they'd given up calling or dropping in on her. As one friend had put it, "If you don't want company, I won't bother you anymore."

She couldn't stay here. What's more, she needed transportation. Dare she return to her condo to retrieve her car? She walked back home, all the while checking over her shoulder. After circling the condo several times, she used the code to her garage and got her car.

She needed help…and the one man who could help her was the same one she'd never thought to see again.

Josh Harvath finished packing his duffel bag. He was taking a much-needed vacation, heading to the warmer temperatures of Arizona. Away from the brutal cold of a Colorado winter. Away from the demands of working for S&J Security/Protection, where he could serve as a bodyguard one day and a computer hacker the next. Away from his mother's meddling in his social life. Away from the pressures of always being on call, whether at work or as an eligible single man whom every aunt, friend and female co-worker had on speed dial.

And though he liked his job and loved his mother and didn't mind serving as the occasional plus-one, he needed to get away. The last year had been a hard one. He'd been wounded while serving as a bodyguard for a visiting member of European royalty and had spent six weeks in rehab. That, plus going undercover as a computer whiz at a high-tech company to ferret out who was selling secrets—and getting his butt whipped along with three broken ribs by the two men intent on not going to prison—had taken its toll. He was back to full strength, but it had been a grueling process.

So when someone pounded on his door with annoying persistence, he was tempted to ignore it. His training and, yes, a dose of curiosity finally kicked in. Who would be knocking on his door today when he'd told everyone he knew that he'd be out of town for a week? If his employers at S&J Security/Protection wanted to contact him, they'd have called his cell. The same for his mother. Was it sad that they were the only people he could think of who might want to get ahold of him?

Though he didn't expect trouble, he kept his Glock at his side. No sense in playing the fool, not when burglaries and muggings had increased substantially in Denver, even in the daytime.

Outside the door stood a woman he'd never expected to see again. The woman he'd walked away from eleven years ago. His body tensed, his heart picking up its beat and stomach clenching. How many times had he told himself to forget her, that it was best they'd gone their separate ways? Not a day went by that something didn't trigger a memory of her, even for a moment. A song. A passage from a book. It didn't matter what.

"Are you going to invite me in?" she asked when he made no move to do so.

He opened the door wider, allowed her to slip past him. "Kylie. What are you doing here?"

"Gracious as ever."

And she was as beautiful as he recalled. Maybe even more so.

There were differences between then and now, slight, but he could see them. Her cheekbones were more pronounced, her once long hair was cut in what he supposed was called a pixie, and her waist, always slender, was now so narrow that he could probably span it with his hands.

But her eyes hadn't changed, dark eyes that seemed to see straight through him. Eyes that had once held tenderness and were now filled with confusion.

He gestured to the sofa and took a chair across from it. "Are you going to tell me what you're doing here?"

She bit down on her lip. He recalled her making the gesture when they were kids, whenever she was about to cry but didn't want to give way to tears.

"Kylie. Tell me what happened."

She shuddered before abruptly standing up as though she'd been scalded. "I'm sorry. I shouldn't have come here, but I didn't know where else to go."

Now he was concerned. Why had she come? "Tell me."

"Someone attacked me in my condo this morning."

"Are you all right?" He pushed the past back where it belonged and barked out the question, the only thing that mattered now.

"I'm fine." But her voice didn't sound fine. It quivered in a very un-Kylie manner.

"Do you know what he wanted?"

"An SD card. He wanted the pictures I took at the governor's speech today."

He nodded, a silent invite to continue.

"I don't know why he wanted it. It's just pictures of the crowd and their reactions."

He'd kept up with Kylie and knew she was an award-winning photojournalist. She'd visited hot spots all over the world. Her photographs caught both the horror and the occasional glimpse of compassion in such places as Ukraine, the Congo and other countries under siege.

Though he'd never admit it to her, he had two of her photos, which he'd scraped up the money to purchase and had hung in his bedroom. Lately, she'd been focusing her attention on the angst in America, on everything from racial strife to public shootings.

"Start at the beginning."

She took him through it step-by-step, including her trip back to her condo to retrieve her car.

"You took a risk going back to your place," he said.

"I was careful, made sure that the creep was gone."

By the time she'd finished, he was more than worried. For someone to break into her condo and threaten her, then demand an SD card, meant that something more serious than merely wanting pictures of a crowd at the governor's speech was going on.

She must have caught something else in her lens, something that was worth killing for.

"Think. Did you see anything, anything at all, that gave you pause when you were taking pictures?"

"Don't you think I haven't asked myself that question?"

That was the Kylie he remembered. Giving as good as she got with a healthy dose of tart thrown in for good measure.

"I don't know," he said calmly. "That's why I'm asking."

"I'm sorry. The whole thing has me rattled." Another un-Kylie thing. The Kylie he remembered would have never admitted to any weakness. She went from fragile to sharp to fragile all within a breath.

His gaze softened. "You have a right to be rattled."

"I didn't know where else to go."

An awkward beat of silence bounced between them.

For her to come to him told him just how frightened she was. When they'd parted so many years ago, he'd never thought to see her again. Angry words and hurt feelings had torn their relationship apart.

"You did right in coming here. How did you know I still lived here?" He'd bought the place from his mother when his dad passed away a few years ago.

"I'd hoped your parents might still be here and could tell me where you were." She gazed at the suitcase. "Were you going somewhere?"

"Not anymore."

"I heard you were working for a protection agency. Thought maybe you could help me find someone to protect me…until I get this sorted out."

"No."

"No?"

"That's right. No. I'll be taking care of you. That's why you came here, isn't it?"

"But we…" She didn't finish.

"Yeah. We didn't part under the best of circumstances." You could say that again. The last time they'd seen each other, he'd ended up walking away. He'd wanted Kylie to come with him to California, where he'd be undergoing SEAL training. His dream for them to marry and have a family remained just that: a dream.

He knew the statistics regarding navy SEALs and marriage, but he was convinced that it would be different for him and Kylie. They were so much in love. How could it not work?

Kylie had had her own dreams, though, and following him to California didn't fit with them. Looking back, he could only shake his head at his selfishness. He'd expected her to drop her dreams so that he might follow his.

They'd gone their own ways. Following a seven-year stint in the SEALs, he'd worked as a US marshal on the East Coast, and had only returned to his home state when he'd received the offer to work at S&J's Denver office.

He'd changed from the self-centered man he'd been back then. But he wasn't going to get into that with Kylie. Not now.

"I don't know what to do." The words were said so softly that he almost didn't catch them.

This wasn't like the Kylie he remembered. She'd always been so sure of herself, of what she wanted, of how she planned to go about getting it. The frightened woman standing before him was vulnerable in a way the Kylie of eleven years ago had never been.

"We'll work it out."

"Will we?"

He was about to reassure her, but the window shattered and the room filled with smoke. A flash-bang.

He grabbed her hand and pulled her into the kitchen. "Stay down." He drew his weapon. And waited.

Kylie didn't like the role of damsel in distress. She didn't like it at all. Like it or not, though, it had been her default role ever since she'd been freed from the prison camp.

So when Josh told her to stay down, she did. And hated herself for it. She then gathered up the tatters of her courage and looked for a way she could help. She knew how to use a gun; in fact, she was more than proficient at it. She'd made a point of learning how to use various weapons after her first assignment overseas. Witnessing warlords attack villagers in the Congo and other war-torn countries had convinced her that she needed to be prepared to take care of herself.

"Do you have another weapon?"

He handed her the Glock he held and grabbed the Sig Sauer he kept strapped at his ankle.

She was familiar with both but preferred the Sig. "Let me have the Sig."

What she didn't tell him was that she hadn't handled a gun since her time as a prisoner.

"Don't fire unless you have to," he said and handed her the weapon.

"Don't worry." She didn't relish the idea of shooting anyone, but she would if it came down to protecting herself and Josh. She'd brought this trouble to his house. How had her intruder found her here?

There'd be enough time to worry over that later. For now, she just wanted to stay alive.

The crack of wood alerted them that the front door had been breached.

Josh put a finger to his lips, then motioned her to head to the pantry. There, he pulled out a bag of sugar and two matches. She got it. Sugar, with its chemical formula, and matches produced a combustible reaction.

"When I give the mark, throw the bag," he said.

He gave the signal at the same moment the bad guys burst into the kitchen. The blinding light and flames shocked the men. In their confusion, Josh managed to disarm them. He handed their weapons to Kylie.

"If either one moves, shoot 'em."

"Gladly."

She kept the gun trained on the two intruders, neither of whom she recognized as her attacker. So there were at least three men involved.

One man, the bigger of the two, got to his knees and glared at Josh. "Quit pointing that gun at me, or I'll show you how smart I am."

Josh knocked him back down. "Stay down if you know what's good for you."

After grabbing a couple of flex-cuffs, he bound their hands. He then undid the men's belts and used them to bind their feet. He clearly wasn't taking any risks they might escape.

She admired his efficiency and, wanting to help, found two dishrags and stuffed them in the men's mouths. One aimed a hate-filled glare at her. She gave as good as she got and glared back at him, having the satisfaction of seeing him lower his gaze.

Josh gave her a short nod after glancing at the rags. "Good thinking. We don't want them yelling for help and attracting the neighbors before the police get here. The longer they stay out of circulation, the better."

He searched the men and came away with a set of earbuds, which he handed to her.

The earbuds seemed to be connected to a cell phone. She listened. "Mackleroy, did you get the card?" The voice thrummed with impatience.

"Mackleroy, Washington, talk to me. Tell me you got it."

When no answer came, the speaker abruptly hung up.

"That's the man who attacked me," she told Josh.

"You're sure?"

"I'm sure." She shuddered. "I'd recognize that voice anywhere."

"These two aren't carrying any identification, not that I expected it. But there's another way to identify them."

Initially the two men had fought against the restraints, but they had given up and sat there, resentment oozing from them.

Josh pulled a device from a drawer, what looked like a digital scanner. With the dishrags stuck in their mouths, the men couldn't even protest when he took their fingerprints and sent off the images.

"Where are you sending them?" she asked.

"S&J. They have the equipment to identify these yahoos if they're in the system. I'll be surprised if they aren't.

"My guess is that they're just hired help." Josh sent a disgusted look their way. "They don't look smart enough to do anything but take orders. And they're probably not very good at that."

When Josh's phone rang, he listened. "Fingerprint report," he told her after hanging up.

It surprised her how quickly the results had come in.

"S&J has access to police databases," he said in answer to her unasked question. "Our boys…" he gestured to the two trussed-up men "…are low-level hoods. Both have served time, but there's no record of who they've worked for in the past. My guess is that they were hired remotely for the job and don't know who's footing the bill."

"What now?"

"We put a whole lot of gone between us and whoever is after you."

TWO

Josh gathered up supplies from the kitchen, focusing on high-energy foods that required little or no preparation.

"There are two sleeping bags in the front closet," he said. "Grab them and any blankets you can find. There's a tarp along with the sleeping bags. Better get that, too." They were going to need them.

"Where are we going?" Kylie asked.

"Away from here."

He threw some winter clothing into his duffel bag. They'd need changes of clothes, and though his would swallow Kylie, they didn't dare go back to her place to get some of her own. She'd have to make do with his. The last thing he grabbed was several lengths of rope.

He looked about and wondered what he had forgotten. Preparation for a trip to the mountains was everything. It could mean having enough to eat or going hungry. More, it could spell the difference between surviving and not surviving.

The warmer temps of Arizona would have to wait.

He wondered what the police would make of the scene. He called S&J and asked that an operative be sent to his house and then contact the police to have the men picked up. It wasn't that he didn't trust the police, but he didn't want to spend the time it would take explaining the situation.

He wanted to get Kylie out of there as quickly as possible. Just as important, he needed to find out how the men had found her.

It could be as simple as they had picked up her tail and followed her, but Kylie had always been street-smart. She would have noticed a tail first thing.

"Let's go," he said and hustled her out of the kitchen door leading to the garage. His big Expedition could handle most terrain. They'd need it where they were going.

"Make yourself comfortable," he said once she was strapped into the vehicle. "It's a couple hours' trip."

"Where're we heading?"

"The mountains. My uncle's got an off-the-grid cabin in Rocky Mountain National Park."

It was her life on the line, and she followed without further questions. Twenty minutes later, they'd left the city behind. The relief of leaving city driving and being on the open road eased the tension in his shoulders, and he was at last able to focus on Kylie.

"You holding up all right?" he asked.

She nodded. "Considering I've had a man threaten my life, two others show up at your place and I'm heading to I-don't-know-where, I'm doing fine." She flushed at the bite in her voice.

"Give the smart mouth a rest, why don't you?" he suggested gently. "We're going to be together for a while."

"Sorry." She ducked her head. "I didn't mean to snipe at you. I guess I'm more rattled than I thought."

"You have a right." He understood Kylie well enough to know that she abhorred being dependent upon someone else. It wasn't in her nature to hand over control. To him. To anyone.

She sighed. "I brought trouble to your door, and now you're paying the price. I should be thanking you rather than picking at you."

"No need for thanks."

"I'm sorry about falling apart on you," she said in a stilted voice. "That's not me. At least, not usually."

"Hey, it's okay. And you didn't fall apart. I'd say you handled things really well, considering."

"Thanks."

She loosened her jacket, revealing bruising around her neck. His mouth tightened, but the marks weren't what he focused on. No, it was the thin gold chain he'd given her eleven years ago. He didn't know she still had it, much less that she continued to wear it.

Not the point, he reminded himself and focused his attention on the bruises. From the look of it, her assailant had had large hands. The man who had put his hands on her would pay.

"Put your head back and try to get some rest," he said.

She sent him an incredulous look, clearly asking how she was supposed to rest when her world had been turned upside down, but she did as he said. Soon, he heard soft, even breathing that told him she had slipped into sleep.

Good.

He had some thinking to do, and he didn't want her peppering him with questions. Kylie had always been curious, wanting to know everything immediately.

It was a good quality for a journalist, and he even admired her for it, but now wasn't the time.

Right now, he had his own curiosity to satisfy and he lined up the questions as best he could.

What had Kylie caught on her camera?

Who wanted the photos?

Why?

And, most important of all, how far were they willing to go to get it?

* * *

Kylie woke, startled to find herself in a truck with Josh Harvath. *What's going on?* When the memory of a man trying to strangle her returned, her breath hitched in her throat.

"You okay?" Josh asked.

"Y…yes." She didn't sound okay and tried again. "Fine."

The doubtful look he sent her way told her that she'd been less than convincing.

She couldn't shake the memory of her attacker's hands around her throat. She'd run from him. The last thing Kylie wanted was to run, but it looked like that was exactly what she was doing. Running.

Worse, she'd run toward Josh—the man she'd left years ago. She glanced at his profile from the passenger seat. She couldn't believe she'd managed to get a few moments' rest on the drive. She felt safe with him.

She'd always felt safe with Josh. Though he'd been scarcely more than a boy when they'd parted, he'd had the same steady air about him, saying that you could count on him.

Admit it, girl. You're scared. She'd faced warring tribes in Africa. Stared down gangbangers in cities all over the world. Even run with the bulls in Pamplona. But knowing that strangers wanted something from her enough to kill her for it took fear to a whole new level.

For seven years, she'd traveled the globe, capturing the world's people on her camera and sometimes her phone. She'd encountered the best in people…and the worst. She thought she'd seen everything.

So much for the intrepid journalist she'd worked so hard to become. Face it. That woman had died in a prison camp halfway around the world. She'd lost the essence of herself and a man she'd grown to care deeply for.

She didn't allow herself to think about Ryan very often. They'd met during a trip to Ukraine. He'd been a war correspondent. Their careers had complemented each other, and they had found they shared much in common on a personal level, as well. After that first meeting, they'd worked together on numerous occasions. With his connections, he was able to pick and choose his own assignments.

When she'd received permission to accompany an NGO to a war-ravaged village in Afghanistan, Ryan had done the same. Terrorists had invaded the village, killing the boys and men and rounding up the young girls. Ryan hadn't been able to stand by while innocent people were murdered, and had fought back. He'd been shot for his trouble and had bled out in front of her.

Scant minutes later, she had been captured along with the villagers and taken to a prisoner camp.

Images of prisoners being abused had imprinted themselves on her mind, refusing to let go, while smells, ripe with raw sewage and molding food and blood, always blood, wound their way through her thoughts.

Horrific memories crossed her mind.

The constant sting of sweat on the wounds that covered most of her body. The cries from other captives. And then the unthinkable had happened. She became so accustomed to them that they no longer bothered her, and that frightened her almost more than anything.

"Kylie?" The sound of her name brought her back to awareness. "Hey, where'd you go?" Josh asked.

"Nowhere."

For a moment, she lost track of where she was.

The look he sent her told her that he recognized she'd sidestepped the truth, but that he wouldn't call her on it. For that, she was grateful.

"Sorry. I must have zoned out for a minute."

"No problem. It happens."

It had been happening ever since she returned from the Middle East. Her therapist said it was the result of trauma, but she'd been back in the States for almost six months. Shouldn't she be over it by now?

The question had taunted her relentlessly, causing her to doubt herself. The hard-earned self-confidence that had seen her through plenty of tough situations had disappeared, leaving a shell of the woman she'd been.

"Hey, it's going to be all right. I'm not letting anything happen to you. That's a promise."

The quiet resolve in his voice settled her nerves. Josh was a man of his word. When he gave a promise, you could count on him to keep it.

He'd been the same when they'd been youngsters together. That was why she'd turned to him even after all the years they'd spent apart. Going to him hadn't been wise. She couldn't afford to fall for him again. Especially not when her sense of self was now so damaged. She was too vulnerable to let him back into her life in any but the most practical sense.

"Thanks." She flushed at her grudging tone. He had gone out of his way to help her, and she couldn't even be gracious. She chalked it up to being terrified. "Seriously. Thank you."

She thought about what had prompted her to go to Josh in the first place. It had been over a decade since they'd parted, but she'd never forgotten him. He had been her first love, but that was over. She could have turned to a friend, but it was Josh's name that appeared in her mind when she'd been threatened.

Needing to change the subject, she asked, "Where are we going? I know you said the mountains, but just *where* in the mountains?"

"A cabin just west of Rocky Mountain National Park. My uncle owns it. Nobody will know we're there. It'll give us time to figure out who's after you and what they think you have on your SD card."

"I keep telling you that I don't have anything but pictures of anonymous faces."

"Maybe you caught some faces that shouldn't be seen…or shouldn't be seen together."

She'd thought of that but hadn't come up with any ideas of who it could be.

"Like who?"

"That's what we have to find out."

Could he be right? She hadn't noticed anything out of the ordinary in the sea of faces she'd captured. The pictures were of people expressing their shock and anger over the latest school shooting and what the governor was going to do about it.

She hadn't had time to go through the photos, especially not with an eye to who might not want his or her picture taken. If someone didn't want to be seen, why attend such an event? To meet somebody? But then why not meet privately? Certainly, that made more sense.

Didn't it?

Maybe that was exactly why individuals who didn't want to be seen together would arrange to meet in a crowd. They would be but two more faces in a mass of faces.

No one would attach any significance to them.

"You could be right," she said slowly, thinking it through.

Josh opened his mouth, but his response was drowned out by a jolt from behind. She turned her head to see a semitrailer barreling straight at them.

There was no question as to who would win in the dogfight that was certain to come. She inhaled sharply, held her breath, and wished she and God were still on speaking terms.

Josh fought to hold the Expedition steady. It was a good-sized vehicle, but the semi that was riding his tail was huge. There was no way he could hold out against it. What's more, the tractor-trailer appeared to have a beefed-up engine that handled the speed they were going with ease.

He had been in high-speed chases before, as a SEAL, then with the Marshals Service and now S&J, and knew what to do. He didn't fight the wheel as his SUV spun but rather steered it in the direction of the spin.

Minutes stretched into what felt like hours before he gained control and gestured for Kylie to take the steering wheel. "Hold it steady while I get a shot off."

"How're you going to do that?"

"Like this."

He pushed the button to roll down the window, pulled himself half out of it and took aim. Maintaining his position and sighting his weapon was a balancing act on its own as the wind tore at him, nearly yanking him out of the window and throwing him to the ground.

Two shots to the engine should do the trick.

Shooting out tires as was shown on every TV cop show ever made wasn't an option. Trajectory and motion were against the shooter every time, but hitting an engine block was doable.

He couldn't hear the ping of the bullet against metal, but the smoke streaming from the semi's engine in angry black billows told its own story. Back at the wheel once more, he could see the truck grinding to a stop.

"Showing off, Harvath?" Kylie asked.

"Doing what was needed."

"You always were a good shot. Even when we were kids you could hit whatever you aimed at."

He and Kylie had whiled away many a summer afternoon honing their shooting skills. There wasn't money to go to a shooting range, and neither could stomach the idea of shooting at wildlife, so cans and bottles it was. He'd become proficient at shooting with either hand. That particular ability had stood him in good stead when he'd made the Teams.

"They won't be going anywhere anytime soon," he said, "but I'm guessing they're on the phone right along now to call in reinforcements."

"How did they know where we were?"

That was a good question.

He'd made sure they weren't being followed, employing surveillance detection routes. The SDRs weren't foolproof, but they normally defeated any but the most experienced of tails. Had he missed something?

No one was infallible.

"Did you stop anywhere on your way to my place?"

"No. I was running for my life." Her wry tone didn't mask the worry in her voice that the bad guys were somehow tailing them.

Was it possible the man who'd tried to choke her had put a bug on her? But that didn't make sense. From what she'd said, the assailant planned to kill her after taking what he wanted from her. Why would he put a tracking beacon on her?

Had he only wanted her to believe that he planned on killing her? But to what purpose?

While he focused on navigating the winter roads, she spent a few minutes checking her clothing but didn't find anything. Nothing about this made sense.

They didn't have time to worry over it; they had to get out of there. Now.

Kylie knew they weren't out of danger. The hard set of Josh's jaw told her more than could any words that he was preparing for the next attack. Even though she was a strong, independent woman who had been taking care of herself since she was eighteen, she was grateful to have him on her side.

She asked what they were both thinking. "How did those men track me?"

Josh's mouth was a tight line of consternation, and she knew he was bothered by the same thing. He avoided the question and said, "We have to keep moving."

"Even if someone is following?"

"Even if."

The question of how the men had found her continued to tumble through her mind, but she had no answer. Why was it so important to someone to get those photographs?

"I smell a story," she said, "though I can't think what it would be. All I did was capture expressions of the people in the crowd. Some were troubled. Many were so full of grief that I could barely bring myself to invade their privacy. I probably won't end up using a lot of the pictures for that reason." That had always been a problem in her work, her unwillingness to use pictures that had captured too much.

"Is there someplace with a restroom near here?" she said a minute later. She needed one. Now. And it wouldn't hurt to check again for a tracking device.

"What's the matter? Can't you use a bush?" The glimmer in his eyes was rich with amusement.

She glared at him. She'd used plenty of bushes in her travels and had gotten bitten, pricked and stung for her efforts. "I can, and I have. I've also used a bucket for a shower and a hole in the ground for a toilet. But I prefer a real bathroom with a real toilet and a real sink if possible."

"Gotcha covered," he said and within ten minutes turned into a rest area complete with restrooms, a convenience store and a fast-food place. "I wouldn't mind using a real restroom myself."

After taking care of business, Kylie patted down her clothing once more. Nothing. She checked her phone for an app that could be tracking her or sending out a signal of her location but again found nothing. She wandered into the small store and purchased snacks for the rest of the trip. Chips, cookies, soft drinks. High energy foods, though they lacked any real nutrition.

Josh emerged from the men's room. "I see you picked up the necessities," he said after peeking into her bag.

"Nothing but the best." She smiled. "Did you want something special?"

"No. Although I did develop a taste for grubs when I was stationed in the Pacific for eight months. They've got a nice crunch to them and are high protein along with it." The crinkle at the corner of his eyes told her he was teasing.

She made a face. "No grubs. But I got chips, and they're crunchy."

The banter felt good after the last tense hours.

Josh looked at the sky and frowned. "There's a storm moving in. We need to get on our way."

While they munched on the snacks, she snuck the occasional glance at him. He was still the same straight arrow she remembered. Over the last eleven years, he'd grown even more appealing, with craggy lines around his eyes and mouth, adding character to his face, and a muscular frame that would make Hollywood hunks envious.

The boy she remembered had been cute. The man was rugged-looking, with leathery skin, no doubt due to long days in the heat and cold of wherever he'd been deployed.

But it was his steady gaze that told her and anyone else bothering to look that he was a man you could count on when trouble came knocking.

"We've got another two hours," he said once they were back in the Expedition and he had checked for bugs. "Talk to me and keep me from going to sleep."

She snorted at that. Josh wasn't one to fall asleep on the job.

"Is there anyone special in your life?" she asked.

"No."

The answer was clipped, bordering on rude.

"Sorry. I didn't mean it to come out that way. But, no, there's no one special. There hasn't been in a long time."

What did he mean by that?

A man like Josh would have dated, could well have married in the years since she'd seen him.

"What about you?" he asked.

"There was someone."

"What happened?"

"He was killed."

The bald words shocked her. She hadn't meant to be so blunt, but the words had come out before she'd thought better of them. She never talked about Ryan's death. The circumstances had been so horrific that she feared she wouldn't be able to get the words out without breaking down in tears.

She didn't say that Ryan had died in her arms while protecting villagers from the terrorists. Or that he had asked her to marry him several times over a two-year span and that she'd never given him an answer. Most especially, she didn't tell Josh why she hadn't accepted Ryan's proposal immediately. And she certainly couldn't tell him that he was the reason.

So she left it at that and hoped he wouldn't pry.

"I'm sorry," he said softly.

"So am I." She might not have loved Ryan as she'd once loved Josh, but she'd cared for him a great deal and had grieved his death. He'd deserved better than to die by the hand of a terrorist who was only a coward at heart and had not an ounce of Ryan's courage and compassion.

Josh was close enough that she could see the gold flecks in his dark eyes. She'd always loved his eyes, so deeply brown that they appeared almost black.

Did he remember how she used to look up to him? He had been a hero in every sense of the word. For that matter, he still was.

He cut short her musings. "You know that the people who want that SD card aren't going to give up, don't you?"

"I know."

"The question is how far do you want to take it?"

"As far as I need to." Her words were put to the test when the Expedition picked up speed and careened wildly down the mountain road.

THREE

Josh tapped the brakes. Mountain driving wasn't a spectator sport. When the road curved sharply, he tapped the breaks and realized he couldn't control the vehicle. As it veered toward a drop-off that descended into a canyon, he pulled the steering wheel in the other direction and stepped on the brakes with everything he had.

He managed to correct the vehicle's direction, but the road's sharp descent caused it to pick up even more speed. With little hope, he tried the brakes again.

"Josh?" Kylie's voice held a question.

"Hold on."

The narrow road was flanked by a sheer cliff on one side and the canyon on the other. Neither looked promising.

He pulled the emergency brake, but it barely put a beat in the Expedition's momentum. He jerked on the wheel as his vehicle veered to the edge of the road again and did his best to muscle it away from the steep cliff.

They were going over. The words of a childhood prayer found their way into his mind as the SUV toppled into the steep canyon. The Expedition tumbled over on itself. The sensation caused waves of dizziness to dance through his head, but he didn't panic. Experience in similar situations had taught him that the dizziness would pass, but as he and Kylie were jerked around, he knew that they were going to be roughed up by the time the vehicle came to rest.

No, it wasn't the light-headedness he feared, but there was a real possibility of injury, and though the Expedition was made for heavy-duty wear and tear, even it might not protect them from broken bones or a concussion. He didn't worry so much about himself as he did for Kylie.

Always Kylie.

He'd promised to take care of her. The idea of her being hurt on his watch was anathema to him.

A hard impact jarred him when the vehicle stopped its wild descent and the airbags deployed. He tasted blood as his teeth bit down on his tongue. Neither he nor Kylie moved for long seconds. They were hanging upside down, only their seat belts holding them in place.

"Kylie? You all right?"

"I think so."

He gave a silent prayer of relief that she hadn't been hurt. "Give me a minute, and I'll get us out of here."

He yanked on the door handle, but the door was jammed shut. He reached for his weapon and, using the Glock's butt, broke the window. A yank on his seat belt confirmed his suspicion that it was also jammed, and he reached for the knife he kept tucked in his boot. After cutting himself loose, he climbed out, careful of the jagged edges of glass. Testing his arms and legs, he found them working and then rounded the vehicle's front end to free Kylie.

Despite her assurance that she was all right, she was pale. Fortunately, the passenger side door worked, and after opening it, he cut away the seat belt and carried her away from the SUV. He didn't expect it to explode—once again that was the stuff of TV shows—but he preferred erring on the side of caution.

He then went back and gathered up their supplies. They'd need the food and other goods they'd brought along. The Expedition was totaled, and he gave a small sigh over the two years he'd saved to buy it, but it wasn't important. Not in the grand scheme of things. What mattered was that he and Kylie were unharmed.

He wanted to lift the hood and check the brake line, but with the vehicle coming to rest on its roof, he couldn't get to it. If he had to guess, he'd say the brake line had been cut.

Someone had deliberately tried to kill them.

Arms full, he went back to where Kylie waited for him. "We've got to get out of here. Whoever did this is going to come looking to see if we survived. If they find we have, they'll want to pick us off. We're sitting ducks where we are." One of the key rules in the SEALs was not to make yourself a target.

They divided the supplies into their bags. If he'd known they'd have to scramble up a cliff, he'd have brought backpacks.

He scanned the cliff they'd have to scale. There was no way they could climb it straight up. They would need to make the climb diagonally. That would take longer, but it would be far safer. As though to punctuate his gut feeling that the men who sabotaged the brakes were coming after them, shots fired in their direction.

He pushed Kylie behind a copse of scrub trees and, after returning fire, followed her. Noises from above alerted him that someone was scrambling down the cliff after them.

"Let's get out of here," he said.

He plotted their course in his mind. If they kept to the far side, they could take shelter from shots in the scrub oak and bushes that dotted the rough terrain.

The first leg of the trip went smoothly enough, and they reached a narrow ledge where they rested for a few minutes. The second leg proved more difficult as the climb grew steadily steeper.

Looking for a handhold, Josh grabbed onto a sturdy-looking shrub. As he tried to haul himself up by it, it proved itself anything but and pulled away from the dirt. He toppled backward and would have fallen, but Kylie grabbed his wrist and stopped his descent.

Lines of strain etched themselves into her face as she fought to keep him from tumbling down the cliff.

He knew she couldn't hold him for much longer. When her hand slipped, he yelled, "Let go." There was no sense in both of them falling. He might survive a tumble down the cliff. He might not. But he wasn't taking Kylie with him. SEALs put their teammates first. Always.

"No." The single word held enough resolve to convince him to not bother arguing with her.

It would take time he didn't have. His free arm flailed wildly until he finally grabbed hold of the edge of a large rock. Once he got a grip on it, she released his other arm, and he pulled himself onto it. He lay there and panted.

That had been close. Too close.

"Thanks," he said once he got his breath back.

"No problem," she answered with a calm that

belied the fact that she'd probably saved his life. Another minute passed before he registered the series of shaky breaths she took.

So she wasn't as casual about the incident as she pretended to be.

They continued the climb and within twenty more minutes of reaching the road, they encountered men scrambling up the cliff. When shots were fired at them, he pushed Kylie behind a thicket of brush and, after returning fire, followed her. After several minutes, he wondered if they'd lost the gunman tracking them or if he'd given up only to try again at a later time.

Josh had no doubt that there would be another time. He tried his cell and discovered he didn't have coverage. No surprise there. He needed to get to a phone and call for help. The gas station/ convenience store where they'd stopped had a phone booth, a rarity in today's world.

They kept to the road's bank in case their pursuers came looking for them. When a truck's engine sounded, they took to the trees in a ditch. It was a little-used stretch of road. What was the likelihood that the truck's driver was just someone who happened to be using the road at that exact time?

Not good.

"The brake line was cut, wasn't it?" she asked as they hunkered down in some scrub oak and brush.

"I can't say for sure, but, yeah, that'd be my guess. Probably when we were in the store."

Cutting a brake line wasn't difficult. All it took was a sharp tool and a little time. The men after them had probably cut the line partway through, making it appear that everything was all right until the fluid ran out. By then, the damage was done and the vehicle left without any braking power at all.

He checked the sky. It had darkened while they'd climbed to the road. They'd be fortunate to hoof it back to the store before it was pitch-dark.

Their gear wasn't made for hiking, but it couldn't be helped. When Kylie lagged behind, he called over his shoulder, "You doing all right?"

"Fine." She jogged a few steps to catch up with him. "You really know how to show a girl a good time."

His lips quirked. "Yeah, I'm known for that."

"I remember."

The two words pulled him back in time to when the two of them had been dating. They'd been so wrapped up in each other that they barely noticed anyone or anything else. That last summer had been filled with such sweet memories that he'd wanted to store them away. Lazy days spent by a lake had invited the kind of sharing between young people filled with dreams and hopes of what they yearned to be.

The quiet hours had been interspersed with waterskiing on the lake and hiking in the mountains. Kylie was a born athlete and always up for a challenge, including climbing some of Colorado's famed mountains.

The days had been touched by a charmed delight that promised a future of happiness and togetherness.

A half smile nudged his lips upward as he thought of how his SEAL teammates and fellow operatives at the Marshals and S&J would razz him if he had ever shared that with them.

The simple joy of that time had come to an abrupt end when he'd asked her to go with him to Coronado to pursue his dream of becoming a SEAL. They had separated, going their own ways, and he hadn't been able to help wondering what would have happened if she'd accepted his invitation.

He pushed the thoughts from his mind and focused on the here and now.

When they felt the first flakes of snow, he prayed it wouldn't turn into more. They'd done all right so far, but getting wet spelled trouble, especially in the mountains.

"Another mile and we'll be there," he said.

He didn't say what they were both thinking: another mile of hiking in the freezing temperatures plus snow would put them in a bad way.

Twenty-five minutes later, they reached the store. Josh found an old-fashioned phone booth tucked near the restrooms and made a call to S&J and asked for a vehicle to be delivered. S&J didn't stint on their employees and helped out whenever they could on personal matters. He watched Kylie as she picked up more snacks and then saw her come to a hard stop.

The look on her face told him something was wrong.

Something was very wrong.

Kylie ducked behind a display of wildlife pamphlets. The man who'd attacked her in her condo stood only six feet away. She'd recognized his smell before she'd seen him.

Her attacker hadn't spotted her. She was certain of that, but if he moved a couple of steps to the right, he couldn't help but notice her.

She sent Josh an urgent look, pointed to the man, then held a hand to her throat. He got the message and motioned her to walk his way. Cautiously, she moved out of the man's line of sight and joined Josh.

He wrapped an arm around her shoulder, and she felt much of the fear-induced adrenaline dissipate.

They exited through the back door. The whoosh of cold air came as a relief to the anxious tension that had gripped her from the moment she'd seen the man.

"Did you see anyone with him?" he asked once she'd assured him that, yes, that was the intruder who had tried to choke her.

She shook her head. "There was a man standing close by who might have been a partner, but I can't say I really saw anyone with him."

"I'd say we found at least one of the men responsible for cutting our brake line."

Cold settled in her gut at his words. Having the SUV tampered with was the fourth time in only a day that someone had tried to kill her. Not for the first time, questions of why they wanted that SD card so much tumbled through her mind.

"What now?"

"We turn the tables on them." The glint in his eyes told her he had something in mind.

"What is it?" She was dirty, tired and more than a little discouraged, but she could feel her fight coming back. She relished it. It was time she took action instead of just reacting to what whoever wanted her dead did.

"When he comes out, we take him. Then we ask questions until he coughs up some answers."

"That's your plan? What if he has a partner?"

"We take him, too."

"After we take them—" and she was feeling

pretty iffy about that "—what do we do with them?"

"S&J operatives will be here in an hour with a new vehicle for us. They'll take him—or them if there're two of them—back to Denver and drop him off at a police station."

"And all we have to do is capture them and tie them up in a bow." She didn't try to hide her skepticism.

Josh sent her a quick grin. "That's it. Hey," he said, apparently picking up on her sarcasm, "we can do this. We survived a semitruck trying to run us off the road and then having our ride go head-over-tail down a canyon. What's taking out a cheap punk or two?"

"You're right." Embarrassed by her doubts, she grinned in return. "We're two tough dudes."

"Tough dudes, huh?" He looked her over. "Never thought of you as a dude. Tough or not."

"Too bad. Right now, that's us." She leaned in. "Tell me the plan."

"Well, it's like this." And Josh proceeded to fill her in.

Ten minutes later, their quarry walked out of the store, alone.

Josh intercepted him with Kylie coming up from behind. She held the gun at the man's back.

"Don't move." Her voice had a decided quaver to it, and she hardened it. "Don't move."

Despite her bragging, the gun felt unfamiliar in her hands. It had been a long time since she'd held one, much less used one. She wondered if she could fire it if she needed to.

The knowledge sat uneasily on her shoulders as her thoughts drifted to the past and she was once more a prisoner. A guard had held a gun to her back as she was doing now. She'd done her best to swallow back her fear, but she'd lost control and had vomited up everything in her stomach. The guard had cuffed her at the side of the head, and she'd been sick again.

Feeling that helpless, that filled with fear, had shaken her belief in herself. And though she'd told Josh that she was confident with a gun, pointing it at someone shook that conviction.

Just hours ago, she'd held a weapon on the two men who had broken into Josh's home and hadn't flinched. That was the thing with PTSD. She never knew when or how hard it would strike. She bit down on her lip, hoping the pain would snap her back to reality.

"Kylie? Kylie? You with me?" The sharp note in Josh's voice yanked her back to the present.

Startled, she looked up. How long had he been calling her name? She stared at the weapon in her hands, a weapon still pressed against her intruder's back. Had she been holding it the entire time? She might have killed the man if she'd been careless, gotten startled, and it had gone off accidentally.

"Kylie. You all right?" Josh asked.

She cleared her throat to buy a moment's time, but the question in his eyes had her squaring her shoulders. "Fine."

"Great." But the worry in his voice gave doubt to the single word. He had his own weapon trained on the man now, so she knew it wasn't concern over him. It was worry for her.

"Walk to me." When she did, he said, "That's right. Give me the gun." Concern was plain in his eyes. "You're sure you're all right?"

She wanted to meet his gaze straight on but couldn't manage it. Instead, she put an extra snap in her voice. "Of course I'm sure."

She had never been less sure of anything in her life.

FOUR

"Keep walking," Josh ordered and directed the man to the far side of the gas pumps. "We have some talking to do." He pulled a pair of flex-cuffs from his pocket, yanked the man's wrists behind him and slipped them on him none too gently.

"You've got no right." Outrage rimmed the man's voice.

"No? Try me. You tried to kill the lady and me." Josh motioned Kylie to stand by his side. "I think that gives us the right."

"I'm sure you remember me," she said. The fiery look in her eyes assured Josh that whatever had happened to her a few minutes ago was now gone and she was back to herself.

Still, he was intensely aware of every move he made, every breath he took. He recognized the signs of PTSD and knew that an abrupt move, an ill-spoken word, could trigger an attack.

He returned his attention to the man, who sent Kylie a grudging glare. "I don't know what you're talking about," the bully said. "And you ain't got nothing to prove otherwise."

She pulled down the collar of her shirt and pointed to her neck. "Does this jog your memory?"

He shrugged.

"How do you feel about picking on somebody your own size?" Josh asked.

"Why don't you mind your business?"

"The lady *is* my business."

"I'm just a hired gun," the thug said with surprising frankness.

"Where's your partner?" Kylie asked.

"He—" Too late, the man stopped. "I don't have a partner."

Josh searched him and found a set of keys. He pushed a button on the fob and was rewarded when a mud-splattered SUV chirped. "We'll wait for a while."

With the temperature steadily dropping, the three of them climbed into the SUV, Josh and the prisoner in the front and Kylie in the back.

Almost an hour had passed with no sign of the partner. Any attempt to extract more information from the man was met with failure, and Josh and Kylie gave up.

When two shiny pickups showed up in the parking lot, he signaled to them. Two men stepped out.

With their prisoner in tow, Josh and Kylie went to meet them.

"About time," Josh said.

"Hey, we got here as soon as we could," Luca Brady, his colleague at S&J, said. "We didn't know you were up in the mountains playing Grizzly Adams."

Josh turned to Kylie. "Boys, this is Kylie Robertson. Kylie, meet Luca Brady and Matt Henley. Two of S&J's finest. Kylie ran into some trouble, and I'm helping her out for a few days."

Kylie stuck out her hand.

Josh tried not to smile when both men shook it with careful restraint, obviously trying not to crush her smaller hand with their much larger ones. They were tough men who used their strength to help others, not to hurt. Their squared-away hair and ramrod straight posture hinted at their military background.

"Thank you both," Kylie said.

"It was our pleasure," Matt replied. "Josh would have done the same if the roles had been reversed."

"I know." She nodded. "Still, thanks."

"This the same trouble you had earlier?" Luca asked Josh.

Josh gave a short nod. "Same kind. This guy—" he pointed to the man in the flex-cuffs "—did his best to choke Kylie to death."

She tugged down the collar of her shirt to show the marks made by bruising hands.

Both operatives sent her attacker dark looks. "We'll take care of this yahoo for you," Luca promised. The tone of his voice said that the yahoo in question probably wasn't going to like their methods.

Josh clapped both men on the backs. "You came through, like always."

"Glad we could help," Luca said.

"Just sorry we didn't get to mix it up more with your playmate," Matt added.

"You get those lowlifes at my place delivered to the police all right?" Josh asked.

Luca slanted him a look. "What do you think?"

Josh grinned. "Thanks. Got another favor to ask. Can you get this goon to the police? I don't want my name out there any more than I can help. Tell them that he's the one who attacked Ms. Robertson."

Luca glanced at Matt. "They're gonna want a statement from her. What do we tell them?"

Josh shrugged. "Anything you want. The important thing is that I get her somewhere safe. I have a feeling this won't be the only man who's looking for her." Kylie needed time to catch her breath and to go through the pictures. She couldn't do either if she was subjected to lengthy questioning by the police. He knew how they worked. They'd want a statement, which they would then pick apart. Though he recognized the tactic as a way to get at the truth, he didn't want to see Kylie put through it. Especially not now after she had just suffered a PTSD episode.

Matt nodded. "Can do, though it's going to take some explaining when we turn in another guy."

Josh grinned. He knew Luca and Matt would come through. "See what you can get out of him before you turn him over to the authorities."

"Not a problem," Matt said, gaze hard as he looked at her attacker. "Men who beat up women deserve what they get."

Josh had no doubt that they would get what information they could from the man.

After handing over the keys to one of the trucks to Josh and each grabbing an arm of their prisoner, Matt and Luca took off.

"I like your friends," Kylie said, watching them go. Their new ride was a beefed-up Ford, not much to look at but plenty of power.

"They're good to have around." Once they were in the truck, he said, "Want to tell me what happened back there?"

She stared ahead, not sure what response to give. She tried for nonchalance. "I pointed a gun at a man's back. No big deal." She could scarcely wrap her mind around the events of the day, much less the last few hours.

His silence told her that he wasn't buying it.

"Nothing happened—" She stopped, admitting to herself that she hadn't fooled him. Not for a minute. She pushed the words out in a rush before she lost her courage. "I couldn't breathe. My vision went blurry. For a minute, I forgot where I was, and then I realized I was having flashbacks to being in the prison camp."

"PTSD." At her nod, he said, "It's nothing to be ashamed of."

"Who said I was ashamed?" She felt heat rushing to her face at the snap in her voice. "Sorry. It won't happen again." She realized there was no way she could promise that and flushed once more.

His gaze found hers. It wasn't probing this time but was filled with compassion. "Don't apologize to me. I've had my share of moments where I didn't know where I was. It takes time."

"You've had PTSD?" She found it hard to believe that a strong man like Josh had ever suffered from it. Since her return to the States, she'd blamed herself for what she saw as a weakness. Could she have been wrong?

"A lot of operators have. We've been trained for being taken captive, surviving torture. You didn't have any training. It's no wonder you're having flashbacks."

"I thought I was over them, but this one came

roaring back like it all happened yesterday. I wasn't always so fragile. Now it seems I jump at my own shadow."

"Don't sell yourself short. You endured more than most people could ever imagine. Being held prisoner for six months is nothing to be taken lightly. Some people never come back from that. Physically or mentally. But you did."

Josh gazed at her with such empathy that she nearly cried. Every cell in her body wanted to hum at the genuine caring she read in his gaze. Crying wasn't going to help her and would probably only embarrass him. When he reached over and squeezed her arm, her first impulse was to pull away.

But she didn't.

She let his hand remain there for long seconds, absorbing the comfort she hadn't known she needed. When she did pull back, it wasn't out of fear, but because she was dangerously close to leaning on him.

While the earlier anxiety and fear had subsided, Kylie still felt the residual effects of the flashback. Her therapist had told her to expect them off and on while she was in the recovery process.

The problem was, she couldn't predict when a flashback would happen. It could come when she was tucked away in her condo and could deal with it in private, in quiet. Or it could come as it had today, when she was in a crisis situation and needed her wits about her.

Post-traumatic stress had already stolen so much from her. Once, a particularly severe episode had left her unable to write and she'd missed a deadline, something she'd never done before. More troubling, though, she was no longer taking pictures in war-torn countries, preferring to stick close to home. To safety. Or so she'd thought.

Her work today consisted mainly of freelancing, selling to various news outlets. Her previous work—taking photos for a paper and working closely with her editor, Bernice Kyllensgaard—had earned her a well-deserved reputation, seeing to it that she had no trouble in earning a living by going out on her own. Bernice had been supportive when she'd decided to go freelance.

She had handled the flashback, perhaps not well, but she'd handled it all the same. She called that progress. So what if she'd been holding a gun at the time. Okay, that wasn't good, but how many times was she going to be holding a gun, anyway?

A flash of macabre humor took her by surprise. If things kept going as they were, maybe more than she thought.

"Must have been some mighty deep thoughts," Josh said.

"What makes you say that?"

"I told you. Your eyes give you away every time." He quirked a brow. "Care to share?"

"Not now." Maybe not ever. "Don't worry. I'm okay."

He didn't call her on the lie.

Josh watched the play of emotions as they chased across Kylie's face. Her features had always been expressive, revealing her every feeling. At that moment, he read fear and a fierce determination not to give in to it.

What had happened to her in that camp? He'd been on several missions with his team to rescue hostages from such camps. After one successful rescue, he was feeling good about a job well done.

Until he interviewed the prisoners.

The hostages, who were missionaries, had come away so physically and emotionally damaged that they hadn't been able to answer any but the most rudimentary of questions. When they had been able to talk, their stories of abuse were heart-wrenching. Though he'd thought himself hardened to even the most horrific of accounts from prisoners, he had been hard-pressed not to bawl like a baby.

What had happened with Kylie? He'd noticed the scars on her hands, which she was even now rubbing, probably unconsciously. Were they a reminder of her time there?

What had made her doubt herself? That wasn't the Kylie he remembered. That Kylie had been ready to take on all comers, to fight to the last breath. This Kylie was unbearably fragile, looking as though she might break at the least provocation.

He wanted to see the feisty glint in her eyes, the one that told him and everyone else that no one was going to get the better of her. That Kylie had believed herself to be invincible. He'd seen flashes of the old Kylie, but the PTSD had stripped her of much of her self-confidence.

It shredded his heart to see her so brittle. She didn't look just rattled. She looked shell-shocked. The adrenaline of the last few minutes had worn off, and now she was crashing. Hard.

He couldn't help darting concerned glances her way, needing to reassure himself that she was all right. For a moment, she'd looked so vulnerable that he longed to wrap her in cotton wool and carry her away from the danger chasing her.

Minutes later, she closed her eyes. Her breathing leveled out. Her lashes swept over her cheeks; her mouth was slightly open, and her hair was tousled.

She was everything he remembered. At the same time, she was more, and despite the attempts on their lives, he smiled briefly, grateful that she was back in his life, if only temporarily.

His smile faded as he acknowledged that they were in trouble. He'd done his best to downplay how worried he was about what she'd gotten herself into. She was now a target.

Having served in the SEALs, where being a target was an everyday occurrence, he understood what it meant. An Afghan warlord had put a bounty on him and two of his teammates when they had taken out a key weapons stronghold. Then there were the terrorists who had vowed revenge upon Josh and his team when they had captured thirteen leaders. Being a target wasn't out of his wheelhouse, but Kylie had no such experience that he knew of.

The men after her were clearly professionals. What's more, they had backup teams to call on. They'd missed, but they would return. He had no doubt of that. His job was to protect her while at the same time figuring out why they wanted her SD card.

Kylie was as sharp as they came, so if she said she didn't know what was on the card, he believed her, but there had to be something there, something worth killing over.

When they found out what that was, it would go a long way to keeping her safe. The temptation to push harder to reach the cabin was great, but he rejected it. An early storm had slicked the roads with a thin sheet of ice, which was nearly as deadly as bullets. He was a pro at winter driving, but he hadn't expected to need those skills in early November.

Playing it safe wasn't normally a SEAL move, but he had precious cargo aboard, and once more he looked over at Kylie.

I'll take care of you, he promised silently. Abruptly aware that he was in danger of losing his heart again, he made another promise, this one to himself. He wouldn't fall for her again.

He couldn't.

When Kylie woke, it took a few moments before she realized where she was. And why. The man in her condo. Men breaking into Josh's home, trying to run them off the road and cutting the brake line. All because of an SD card. An SD card that was important for reasons she didn't understand.

From the moment the intruder in her condo had wrapped his arm around her neck, events had moved at warp speed.

"You snore," Josh said.

Denial was swift. "Do not."

"Don't worry. It was cute, just a puff of air with a little gurgle at the end."

"Why didn't you wake me?"

"Why? It made me smile."

"How far away are we from your uncle's cabin?"

"Not far now."

She stretched, then wet her lips. Her mouth was dry. "Are you sure this is a good idea?" she asked. "I mean running away instead of investigating what's going on."

"We need a place to regroup, a place where you can look at the pictures you took. Once we learn what they show, we can start making plans."

"What if we don't discover what it is they're after? I took hundreds of pictures today. None of them stood out."

"Then it's a good thing that you have a second pair of eyes."

Josh had always been practical. She was counting on that now. "Okay. After we find out what those men are after, what then?"

"Then we investigate."

"Call in the police?"

"We can," he said, but he sounded doubtful. "Or we can investigate on our own. You're a journalist. I work for a security firm. Between the two of us, we should be able to dig up what we need."

"Is there some reason you don't want to call in the cops?"

He hesitated, then said, "One of my buddies ran into a case a while back where the cops were as dirty as the bad guys." His eyes darkened.

"What happened?"

"He died because he trusted the wrong person. Turned out to be his police contact."

"I'm sorry," she said quietly.

"Then there was the Lawson case," Josh said, naming one of the biggest cases ever tried in Colorado. "He had more cops on the payroll than a precinct station."

She recalled the notorious case where Douglas Lawson had been found guilty on multiple counts of murder, attempted murder, money laundering, human trafficking and a host of other crimes and was now serving several consecutive life terms in a federal prison.

"I thought Lawson and his people, including a bunch of dirty cops, were all brought in."

"They were. But who's to say there aren't more out there?"

"Okay. I trust you." She flushed at that and averted her gaze. Eleven years ago, they had broken up because she hadn't trusted that they could have a life together.

"Thanks." His smile was wry, as though he knew what she was thinking and was amused by it.

"I don't know if I've really thanked you for dropping everything to help me." It was a struggle to get the words out, but she had to say them. It was bad enough owing him, but it would be far worse if she was ungrateful, as well.

Josh had always been a stand-up guy who was ready to lay it on the line to help a friend. She could hardly be termed a friend anymore, but he hadn't hesitated. Why hadn't she appreciated that about him years ago?

The answer was simple enough. She'd been young and eager to start her own career. At the time, her path had seemed so separate from his... but maybe she could have pursued her dream of being a photojournalist anywhere. Including Coronado, California, where SEAL training took place. There was no point thinking on that now.

"What did you think I'd do?" he asked.

"The same thing you're doing. I guess that's why I came to you in the first place. You were the one person I knew I could count on."

He studied her for a moment. "Hey, it's okay. You're not alone."

"Thank you." That was the only thing she could think of to say.

She felt as awkward as a middle school girl talking with a boy she liked but didn't want him to know it. *Grow up, girl. You're almost thirty years old.* Men didn't intimidate her. Even a man as good-looking and self-assured as the man she'd given her heart to so many years ago.

At that time, he had been everything to her. With her home life a shambles, she had relied on Josh in countless ways. He was strong, confident and so certain of his path in life, while she floundered in making the slightest decision. She'd turned to him repeatedly, until she feared she was losing herself. It had been then that she'd made the decision to pursue her own path. A journalism teacher in her senior year of high school had sparked her interest in photojournalism.

Now she was running back to him, wanting him to solve her problem, and felt that she hadn't made any progress at all. Disgust with herself had her throat closing up.

She'd grown since then. Grown in knowing who she was and what she wanted. She no longer needed someone to lean on as she'd once leaned on Josh, but there was more. The risk to her heart if she let him into it again was too high. Far too high.

Yet the butterflies in her stomach, the hands that clenched and unclenched, were mute evidence that she wanted to lean *against* him. To feel his arms around her.

It was nonsense, of course. The events of the last twelve hours had scrambled her thinking until she wasn't sure of anything.

She needed to remember who she was—Kylie Robertson, award-winning photojournalist. She had survived a deadly fever in the Congo, tribal wars in Afghanistan and six months in a prison camp. If that hadn't broken her, nothing would.

She closed her eyes to regroup her rambling thoughts. She needed to keep her mind on the present.

They took turns driving. Josh took the last leg of the trip and shortly before midnight pulled into a narrow road that led to a rough driveway. At the end sat a ramshackle cabin that looked like it had seen better days, but it appeared sturdy enough and would provide a place for them to rest.

Josh pulled his truck to the back of the cabin out of sight.

The cabin was a simple structure with four rooms, the only heat coming from the woodstove. Amenities included a tiny bathroom and kitchen.

After cleaning up in the bathroom's minuscule sink and, pleasure of pleasures, brushing her teeth with the extra toiletries Josh had packed, she felt ready to face what came next.

She'd made do with a lot less. What mattered was that she felt safe. That had more to do with Josh's presence than the cabin itself.

"It's not much," Josh said.

"It's fine." Life was too fragile to complain about small inconveniences. And if she had to make do with sleeping in a cabin that was heated only by a wood-burning stove, she'd do so. "Compared to some of the places I've stayed, this is a palace."

"Same here." He grinned. "SEALs can't afford

to be picky about their accommodations. I spent more than one night curled up in the branches of a tree, trying to stay out of sight of the guerillas looking for us. When I woke up one morning, I found a snake staring at me."

"What did you do?"

"Stared right back at him."

"You're making that up," she accused.

"Maybe a little."

Appreciating the story and him, she laughed, knowing he'd told her this to lighten the mood.

Josh rejected her idea that they look at the pictures first in favor of eating. With her stomach making impatient noises, she agreed.

From his duffel bag, he pulled out an assortment of canned goods. "What about beef stew?"

As though in answer, her stomach rumbled again. The rumble turned to a growl. Embarrassed, she placed her hand on it.

"When was the last time you ate?"

She had to think about it. "You mean besides the snacks?" At his nod, she said, "Before going to hear the governor."

"No wonder you're hungry. Let me heat this up."

Fifteen minutes later, he was ladling stew into chipped bowls.

When she took her first bite, she nearly sighed her pleasure. "It's the best stew I've ever tasted."

"It comes from a can," he reminded her.

"Doesn't matter," she said between bites.

When they'd finished and cleaned up, he said, "Now we look at those pictures."

She brought them up on her laptop.

Nothing stood out or appeared unusual. Just a sea of faces. She'd gotten a few close-ups, capturing the angst on one, anger on another. That was to be expected. The governor had spoken on an emotionally loaded topic.

Josh had been deployed in Afghanistan, Croatia and Ukraine along with a number of other hot spots and had seen the worst the world had to offer, but the shootings in his own country had shaken him in ways he'd never imagined.

Flanking the governor were huge screens depicting pictures of victims of violence. When a child's face was shown, Josh heard Kylie's mew of pain. He studied her while she gazed at the picture, saw the taut lines bracketing her mouth. Her eyes were dry, but he knew tears were close. From the tight grip in which she held her hands, he knew she was doing her best to keep her emotions in check.

She shouldn't have been embarrassed at her reaction. He'd seen similar pictures, had even witnessed the actual shooting of children, as had she, he knew, but it never got easier. If anything, it only got harder. You thought you got inured to it, but that was a lie. And he realized he didn't want to become desensitized to such images. To do so would mean he'd lost the ability to feel.

He turned his attention back to Kylie when she said, "Weapons are available to anyone who decides they want to shoot up a grocery store, a mall, even a church. In the governor's speech, he talked about how kids think they're invincible. Their brains aren't yet fully formed, yet they're able to get their hands on these weapons and destroy the lives of others as well as their own." Kylie shook her head. "He gave a description of the problem, but nowhere in his speech did I hear a solution."

She blinked several times, an attempt to hold back the tears he knew were threatening.

He pretended not to notice and waited until she was able to speak.

"Don't worry about me. I've seen pictures of children killed by violence and the anguished faces of parents before." Her voice was steady. Somehow he'd have preferred it if she'd given way to her feelings. He didn't want her to have to exercise such tight control over herself. Not with him.

They turned their attention back to the screen, where pictures of children and parents and grandparents predominated. Some carried signs saying "Protect our children." Faces filled with anger were interspersed with expressions of unimaginable grief.

A child's face filled the screen. He couldn't have been more than three or four years old. The bewilderment in his eyes was as heartbreaking as the grief on his mother's face when the shot switched to her. She held a sign showing a picture of an older boy with the caption "He was only seven." It didn't take much guessing to know that the boy would never make it to eight.

A heavy presence of police reinforced the grim subject of the conference.

Josh sat up straighter as another image appeared on the screen. "Go back," he said as she scrolled through the pictures. "There. Look."

She focused in to better see the persons involved.

There, in the corner of one of her photos... Colorado's lieutenant governor was in close conversation with the biggest mob boss in the state.

FIVE

That couldn't be right. Granville Winslaw, the second-highest official in the state government, couldn't have business with George McCrane, the boss of Colorado's biggest organized crime organization, but there they were. Heads together, bodies leaning into each other. The picture hinted of a confidential meeting.

This was no accidental encounter.

She and Josh stared at two people who shouldn't have been together. The two men stood in the shadow of a doorway, partially out of sight, but they were plain enough for her to see. Was it only by coincidence that her shot caught them standing side by side? No, they were obviously talking, and, from the expressions on their faces, not very amicably.

She looked more closely, saw an envelope being passed from McCrane to Winslaw. No, this was not an unintended happenstance.

"What are the lieutenant governor and a mob

boss doing together?" she asked. "And why didn't I see it earlier?"

"You were taking pictures of the crowd, right?" At her nod, he continued, "You weren't zeroing in on any one person."

"I was trying to capture emotion. To understand the story of real people with real grief. So, yes, I was looking at the people, but only to identify expressions."

"They wouldn't have stood out to you then. They were just two men talking."

"Are you patronizing me?"

"No. I'm trying to get you to give yourself a break. It's no wonder these men want the SD card. They'd want anything that puts them together."

Of course the lieutenant governor couldn't afford to be seen with a well-known mobster, especially since she'd heard that he was considering running for governor next term. Why were they meeting here? Hers wasn't the only camera at the event.

"McCrane has his hand in every corrupt enterprise in the state," Josh observed. "Probably the whole Southwest."

She nodded, thinking of how far the man's interests extended, including embezzlement, drugs, money laundering, fraud, gaming, human trafficking, prostitution and more. Though charges had been brought against him numerous times, none had ever been made to stick.

Slick lawyers and a seemingly unlimited supply of money saw to it that he had never seen the inside of a prison cell. Witnesses, those who hadn't been killed or disappeared, had changed their testimonies or refused to testify altogether. And who could blame them? There had been talk of cops and even district attorneys being complicit with McCrane's organization, looking the other way when his name was linked to a crime.

"Why meet in such a public setting?" she said aloud this time, more to herself than to him. "It's like they're asking to be spotted."

"A public setting is exactly the kind of place that two people wanting to keep their meeting a secret might choose."

She tried to make sense of that. "How so?"

"Because most people won't ordinarily notice two people together in a crowd, but put them alone in an out-of-the-way spot, it's like hanging a big neon sign around their necks and announcing that they have a secret."

"Okay. I get that. It still doesn't answer the question of why those two men would be together in the first place." The idea of Winslaw and McCrane working together was beyond terrifying.

Josh smiled grimly. "I'm guessing it's not to plan the next church bake sale."

She almost laughed at the idea of the LG and the state's biggest crime boss planning a church bake sale.

What did Winslaw have to offer? He was a relative unknown in the political field, sent on ribbon-cutting ceremonies and other negligible assignments by the governor. He had a reputation of putting his foot in his mouth and then leaving it there. Because of that and his lackluster appearance, he was frequently the butt of jokes.

She went back to her original question: Why should McCrane want to meet with Winslaw? The LG didn't have the juice to do much, so it wasn't like he could help the mobster out of a jam. And why should Winslaw agree to meet with McCrane in the first place?

Did McCrane have something on him, something to use as blackmail? And if so, what was it, and more importantly, what was he forcing the lieutenant governor to do?

Another thought occurred to her. Maybe McCrane didn't have to force Winslaw to do anything. Maybe Winslaw was in it for the oldest reason in the world: money.

Some said the governor had made a mistake in making Winslaw his running mate. Others said that the state's top official had known exactly what he was doing, that Winslaw made him look good by comparison. Whatever the reason, he held the second-highest position in the state. Despite his ineffectual manner, his presence carried some weight.

"I need to take this to the authorities," she said. But how was she to get it to the right authorities? How far did the corruption go? Police, judges, state attorneys?

She voiced the question aloud. "How do I know who I can trust?" If the lieutenant governor was chummy with a crime lord, it stood to reason that there could be others down the line in state government who were on the take, as well.

Another thought occurred to her. "Do you think the governor's involved, too?"

"I don't know."

The frustration in Josh's voice mirrored her own. They had too many questions and no answers to go with them.

"What would the lieutenant governor want with the biggest crime boss in Colorado?"

"It's more like what would the biggest crime boss in the state want with the lieutenant governor," Josh said.

The journalist in her itched to write the story, but there wasn't a story. Not yet. All they had was a picture of Winslaw and McCrane with their heads bent together.

"We need more," she said, her investigative instincts taking over, "before we take this to anyone. We'd be laughed at out loud if we went to the authorities with what we have now." She knew that, given time, she could dig up the story. If she could take hard evidence to the police, there was a chance this might not get swept under the rug like other crimes surrounding McCrane had.

"You're right. That's why we're going to find out everything we can about Winslaw."

"What about McCrane?" she asked.

"Him, too. But the key here is Winslaw. Maybe he was being blackmailed by McCrane, and when they got to talking, the two of them decided they could do better as partners than enemies."

She considered that theory. "If Winslaw's elected, McCrane has the fast track to get legislation passed that would benefit him... You don't seem very surprised."

"It had to be something like this," Josh said. "I just didn't know the players."

"You must've seen a lot in your line of work."

"More than I wanted to." His tone told her that he'd rather forget much of what he'd witnessed over the years. She felt the same. While she'd observed many acts of true Christian service in her travels, she'd also witnessed scenes of such pain and despair that she'd wanted to wash her eyes out with sand, hoping the grit would remove the images.

Mothers and children, even infants, sent to refugee camps that had no running water, little food and no electricity. That was, if they were fortunate. Too many were slaughtered in the name of revolution, which was really just another term for war.

Her camera had captured too much misery, too much anguish. When she'd returned to the States after her time in the Afghan prison camp, she'd found yet more killing and senseless violence in her own country. When did it end?

Or did it?

She'd been disheartened by today's speech, to see that nothing had changed to end the violence in the nation. Politicians gave glorified speeches while children died and parents wept.

Normally a subject like this would motivate her to create change, but instead, she felt tired and scared. Part of her wanted to retreat from the story. That wasn't like her. It wasn't like her at all.

She turned to Josh, wanting to explain, to apologize. Could she tell him of the horror of being in a prison camp for six months, of witnessing acts of such cruelty that she'd been brought to her knees?

But the words didn't come. Instead, she felt a tear, then another, trickle down her cheek.

"Hey, it's gonna be all right," he said.

"This isn't who I am." It was important he knew that, more important that she said it. The tears came harder, faster. She gave a furious swipe at her eyes. "I hate crying. I ugly cry."

"I don't see anything ugly," he said softly. "I see a woman who's been through a lot of bad stuff and is still going through it.

"You're strong and smart, but even the strongest and the smartest of us can have a breaking point. I'm thinking that after you were rescued from the prison camp, you came home and scarcely gave yourself time to recover. Then you jump right into the whole violence thing that's taking place all over the country. You didn't give yourself time to decompress. You were hurting. Physically and emotionally."

He was right.

She'd seen a therapist but had still waded right into the next assignment without taking the time to process what she'd endured overseas. Right now, she could feel the return of the horror of what she'd witnessed and undergone.

She'd seen far too much of it to be surprised; yet, the calculated cruelty she'd witnessed in the camp had shaken her to her core. Then there were the injuries to her hands. The doctors had warned her that she might never regain total movement. Physical therapy had helped, but the tendons had been damaged to the point that her fingers were still constricted and ached after prolonged periods of use.

And covering stories about the suffering throughout America only affirmed what humanity was capable of.

Josh gave her a one-armed hug, which should have been a perfect blend of comfort and support, but she jerked away. She didn't want to lean on him. Not now. She was only beginning to reclaim the woman she'd been before her capture. She couldn't jeopardize that.

Embarrassed at her response, she made a show of pulling her coat more tightly around her. In wrapping herself in the coat, she noted a smudge at the side. She rubbed at it, frowning when she discovered it was sticky to the touch.

She could have picked it up at any number of places since this morning—had it only been this morning?—when she'd run from her condo. Still, she couldn't place what the smudge was and where she'd gotten it.

The down coat was a new one, a splurge for herself after selling a series of photos to *National Geographic*.

"Wait," Josh said. "Don't rub it." Gingerly, he touched the spot. "I think we figured out how the bad guys have been tracking us."

She looked at the smudge. Was Josh saying what she thought he was? "What is it?"

He frowned. "It's a very high-tech tracking device. All someone has to do is rub a bit on their fingers and then touch something the person they want to track is wearing. The nylon shell of your coat is perfect."

"You're kidding, right?"

"Afraid not. This is the cutting edge in tracking. I think your attacker knew the stakes of getting you and that card. This was his backup plan if he failed." The expression in Josh's eyes turned grim. "Whoever put this in action had access to the latest in military technology, plus a whole lot of money."

"How much money are we talking about?" Her chest tightened and her throat closed; along with it, a sinking feeling settled in her stomach.

"More than you or I make in a lifetime."

Josh took his knife from its sheath and cut away the piece of fabric containing the device and then tossed it in the stove.

"We've got to get out of here," he said. "We can't afford to wait until they track us down again."

The rumble of an engine caused her to go on alert.

Josh did the same, turning toward the window. "Too late. Get on the floor." He pulled aside a curtain and peered outside. "An SUV is blocking the driveway."

"At least we know how they found us." But that was scant consolation in the circumstances.

"We have to move and move now if we're going to get out of here with our skins intact."

She knew there wasn't a back door. She could climb out the bedroom window, but Josh was too big to fit. "What do we do?"

Two shots took out the front windows, followed by two Molotov cocktails being thrown inside. The cabin's all-wood interior swiftly ignited. Smoke and flames filled the cabin. As the smoke thickened, she struggled to breathe.

"Grab your bag," he said. "Don't forget the SD card."

She groped her way to where she'd left her bag and stuffed all that she could inside.

Josh began running his hands over the rough pine flooring and she wondered what he was doing. Now wasn't the time to go looking for dust bunnies. Seconds later, he stopped and pressed his fingers against the floor. A large square of wood came up.

A trap door.

She didn't need Josh to tell her what to do next. She tossed her bag into the darkness. With more speed than grace, she scrambled down two steps carved into the ground. There wasn't room to stand upright, so she sat back on her haunches as she waited for Josh. The air was colder here, and she shivered violently.

He threw his duffel bag down and jumped to

the floor, grunting as he did. A sharp gasp of pain alerted her that he'd hurt himself.

"Are you all right?" she asked.

"Fine." But he didn't sound fine. He didn't sound fine at all.

She started to ask him what had happened when he pulled a rope attached to the door, closing it. The blackness was complete, and she had no idea which way to go.

"This way," he said.

After she slung her bag over her shoulders, she did her version of a military duckwalk as she navigated her way through the narrow tunnel. Her thighs burned with the effort, but it was better than crawling over the cold ground that would seep through her clothes and leave her colder than ever.

Josh followed.

The air grew cooler, and she knew they were no longer under the cabin. "Where are we?" she whispered.

"West of the cabin. Uncle Hal was a conspiracy theorist. He built the tunnel in case enemy forces came after him. The family used to tease him about his 'forces.' Turns out he was pretty smart after all."

Each of Josh's words seemed to come with an effort. "You're sure you're all right?"

"I told you, I'm fine. So leave it." The sharpness of the order convinced her that something was definitely wrong, but she didn't press it. Not now when they were making their escape.

When the roof of the tunnel abruptly lowered, she got to her hands and knees, her progress hampered by dragging her bag behind her. With no light, she was dependent upon touch. The walls felt like they were closing in on her, causing her to stop.

From the time she'd been a small child and had fallen into a toy box and couldn't get out, she'd suffered from claustrophobia and now shivered as much from fear as from the cold. She tried to swallow the lump that was stuck in her throat, but it refused to go down. How did she tell Josh, a man who had never been afraid of anything, that she couldn't move and that she was afraid that the PTSD would kick in at any moment? If that happened, she'd be totally useless.

"Breathe slowly," Josh said. "You're okay. I'm right behind you. If you need to stop again, we'll do it."

His voice steadied her, and she dragged in breaths of stale air. She knew they couldn't afford to stop repeatedly while she dealt with her fears. They needed to get out of there before the men discovered she and Josh hadn't died in the fire.

They kept at it until the tunnel sloped upward. Digging her fingers in the dirt, she pulled herself out. Fresh air filled her lungs, and she breathed deeply, not caring that the air was so cold it felt like shards of glass were filling her lungs.

While they had been clawing their way out of the tunnel, the storm had worsened. Moonlight shimmered over mysterious snow-covered shapes. The eerie effect unnerved her until she realized the shapes were only dead trees, fallen branches, boulders. Every step had to be painstakingly maneuvered over and around the lumps.

She fell twice, tripped by branches hidden in their cloaks of snow.

"Careful," Josh said as he helped her up. "We don't want any broken bones."

"How far are we going?"

"As far away from those clowns who set the cabin on fire as we can." Though he had his phone, there was no service here.

They were on their own.

Navy SEAL training had included a wilderness survival course. The biggest takeaway was the Rule of Three. You could survive three minutes without oxygen. You could survive three hours without shelter in extremely harsh conditions. You could survive three days without water. You could survive three weeks without food.

Right now, it was the shelter component they had to address. They needed to get out of the snow that was falling with no sign of stopping. Wet clothes would send their body temperatures plummeting plus steal the remainder of their rapidly depleting energy. They had been tramping through the snow for close to two hours, and though he could keep going, he didn't know that Kylie had that kind of stamina.

He looked about and spotted a clearing big enough for what he had in mind. "Come on," he said. "We're going to build a lean-to."

Finding poles came first. Using his knife, Josh stripped the poles of their branches and set them aside. He and Kylie then set about intertwining the branches together.

It was painstaking work, especially in the cold, to weave branches in and out. Fingers awkward in gloves, they managed to weave a covering of sorts. When it was large enough, they attached it to the poles with the lengths of rope he'd brought with him. The tarp in his pack would do nicely for ground cover. In less severe weather, he'd have used it for overhead protection, but he feared it wouldn't hold up in the heavy fall of snow, and they needed something to keep the coldness of the ground from seeping into them.

"Our room awaits," he said, gesturing to the primitive shelter.

"It's perfect." Kylie sank to the tarp-covered

ground. "I didn't know how tired I was until we stopped running."

Before he could respond, an explosion lit the air, sparks raining down like a Fourth of July fireworks celebration. Ordinarily, fire in the mountains raced over the land with terrifying speed, but it couldn't get a start in the snow.

"What was that?" she asked.

"At a guess, I'd say the men who set the cabin on fire just blew up our truck." So much for his plan to circle back and retrieve it.

The expression in Kylie's eyes said she'd had the same thought and understood the implications of being stranded with no vehicle.

"Get what rest you can," he said. "Tomorrow, we move. We have to work our way back to some kind of civilization."

He didn't add that their circumstances were more than grim. They had a few power bars, a couple of bottles of water and only the clothes they were wearing. If they hadn't had to flee from the cabin so abruptly, they could have better stocked their bags with supplies he'd brought from home. As it was, they were at the mercy of the elements.

About to shut down his flashlight to save the battery, he saw the blood on his pants, remembering how he had snagged his pants on a nail while he was getting into the tunnel. The incident came into focus as he recalled the sting of the pain when he'd landed on his knee in the tunnel. He hadn't paid much attention to it at the time— he'd been too busy escaping before succumbing to the heat and smoke—but the nail must have pierced the flesh.

"What is it?" Kylie asked.

"Nothing. Just a cut."

While she held the flashlight, he searched for the first aid kit he kept in his duffel bag. It wasn't big, but it held the basics. After making a slit in his jeans, he tended the wound the best he could.

It wasn't a cut after all but a puncture and deeper than he was comfortable with. Puncture wounds could turn nasty if not treated immediately. When he had finished cleaning it, he put liquid stitches on the wound to hold the skin together and bandaged the wound. That should take care of it.

He hoped.

Kylie made a trip behind a copse of trees. What she wouldn't give for a roll of toilet paper.

After taking care of business, she did her best to clean her hands in the freshly fallen snow. That would have to do.

She returned to the camp and lay down on the tarp. Though she willed herself to sleep, the rest she so sorely needed refused to come. Her body had finally stopped shivering, but her mind spun in a thousand directions. What were the lieutenant governor and the mobster meeting about? It had to be something big; otherwise, they wouldn't have gone to such lengths to get the flash card.

When no answer came, she set it aside to wonder how much time she and Josh had before the men trying to kill them realized they weren't inside the cabin and started out after them.

Could they afford taking the time to rest? She was about to ask him, when he said, "It's going to take some time for the fire to stop burning in the cabin and the men to get inside. Then it'll take more time for them to realize that there aren't any bodies. Eventually, they'll find the trap door and follow the tunnel until they come to the opening."

"And after that?"

"They'll be on our tails. We'll have to hustle come morning, but we needed to get out of the storm for the night."

"How did you know what I was thinking?" she asked. The idea that he knew what she was thinking was unsettling, reminding her of their past. He'd often been able to anticipate her feelings and concerns and knew just how to respond. The irony was that she had no idea how to respond now.

"Because I was thinking the same thing. We're okay to rest for a few hours. We're going to need it.

"In the Teams, we learned to sleep when we can because we never know when we'll get the next opportunity."

"Smart."

"Yeah. I know your mind's racing, but let it slow down."

The low timbre of his voice soothed her sprinting thoughts until she was able to shut off her worry.

To her surprise, the next time her eyes drifted shut, they stayed that way. She surrendered to the rest she desperately needed… Until a startling sound had her waking and bolting upright.

SIX

The sound of a truck engine, a low sputter growing into a throaty growl, was unmistakable. Josh berated himself for not getting up earlier. His leg had kept him awake for much of the night. When he had finally given in to exhaustion, he'd slept fitfully. He'd planned to have him and Kylie on their way far earlier. Now the bad guys were closing in.

"Grab your stuff," he said. "We're getting out of here."

His leg was bleeding badly, but there was no time to treat it.

"Your leg—"

"It'll be fine."

The engine stopped, signaling that the truck couldn't penetrate the woods any farther.

In a perfect world, they'd have erased all signs of their presence, but their world was far from perfect. Thrashing noises as their pursuers tromped through snow told him that even now they were headed his and Kylie's way. From the sounds of it, there were at least two, possibly three.

There was no time to dismantle the lean-to, including repacking the tarp. Having to leave it and the rope behind was a blow. He and Kylie barely had time to grab their bags before the men were upon them.

A throbbing ache had settled in his leg. He ignored it and, grabbing Kylie's hand with his left, pointed with his right. "See that stand of pines? That's our goal."

She sent a disbelieving look his way. "That's a good hundred yards away, and you're hurt—"

"Forget about that. We have to move and *move now*."

Uncaring about the noise they made, they ran. They could make it, he told himself. Kylie had run track in high school, and he was in tip-top physical condition. Or, he had been before injuring his leg. He couldn't worry over it now.

The human body was equipped with automatic survival mechanisms, one of the most important being the release of adrenaline. At the first sign of threat, the body released the chemical before parts of the brain even registered the danger.

Adrenaline levels spiked as the body prepared for one of two choices. Fight or flight.

Right now, his body readied itself for flight. His energy surged, telling him he could do this.

The frigid mountain air seared his lungs, but he didn't stop.

He couldn't.

Frost had covered everything with a quiet glow that looked almost ethereal. Kylie wanted to revel in the beauty that only nature could provide but knew that they didn't have the luxury of that.

Gunshots chased them.

They had to keep moving. When bullets sprayed the air around them, Josh threw her to the ground and covered her body with his own. His large frame felt invincible, but no matter how strong he was, he was no match for a bullet.

Something was off with Josh. Last night, he had dismissed the injury to his leg, and she'd gone along with it. This morning, though, the wound was bleeding again. Moreover, his face had an unhealthy sheen to it. She'd seen that before in her line of work—it was fever. Fever had its own flush.

She knew he wouldn't appreciate her asking about it, especially when they were running for their lives, but the first opportunity she had, she'd get the truth out of him. She doubted he'd bring it up, stubborn as he was. That was something that hadn't changed about him.

When they reached the pine trees, they took long breaths, and she waited for him to say something. They had to come up with some kind of plan if they were to evade the men who were after them.

The only problem was that they had only what they carried with them. Scratch that. Of course that wasn't the *only* problem. The weather was worsening, and even though the snow had stopped, the temperature had dropped.

The cold, coupled with extreme exertion, spelled trouble. They were burning up calories at an alarming rate and had only the most meager of rations with no way to replenish them, but they dared not stop to eat.

Josh stumbled. His labored breathing told her that he needed rest.

He slumped a bit, and she looked more closely, noting that the dark crimson stain on his pants leg had spread.

The wound he'd dismissed had bled enough to soak through the leg of his pants. She'd known it was bad, but how had she not known just how truly bad it was? As if things could get any worse. She nearly started crying but held back the tears. The last thing Josh needed was her going to pieces.

"Why didn't you say something?" she asked.

He gave a lopsided smile. "We couldn't stop. Not then."

"Fool." But her hands were gentle as she helped him to the ground. She'd have given her right arm for some kind of cover. A blanket. The tarp they'd had to leave behind. Something.

"Don't worry," he said. "It's so cold that it won't bleed much."

She pointed to the leg of his pants. "You call this not bleeding much?" It was all she could do not to rail at him.

"We had to keep going," Josh said. "We have to keep moving now. They're almost on us."

"When were you going to tell me how bad your leg was?" she persisted.

"It's not important."

She shot him an impatient look. "Of course it's important. How do you expect to run when you're bleeding like that?"

"The only thing that matters right now is keeping ahead of whoever is after us. I can't afford to pamper my leg." The annoyance in his voice told her to back off.

He pulled a compass from his pocket. "We need to keep heading south."

And then what? But staying one step ahead of the men after them didn't leave time for questions.

Only running.

* * *

Josh knew he was in a bad way. His breathing was growing shallower by the minute. His leg ached abominably. He felt Kylie glance at him more and more often. She understood the danger of infection just as he did.

"We've got this," she said.

"Yeah. We do."

It was too bad neither one of them had been able to put any confidence in their voices.

He stumbled over a branch, and she propped him up. He was too big to use her as a crutch. Though she was tall, she was slender.

He turned to the Lord. *We need Your help. Please give me the strength to keep going.* Though he uttered the words silently, he knew the Lord had heard them.

When you think you can't take another step, try for half a step. But keep moving. His drill instructor's words resounded in his mind when the desire to give up crept in and discouragement sat heavily on his shoulders.

You're a SEAL, he told himself. It was time he started acting like one.

"What's wrong?" he asked when Kylie held up a hand motioning for silence.

"There's movement ahead," she said. "I don't know how long we can remain going in this direction."

"So they found us." He didn't waste energy on worry. "It had to happen eventually."

"Yeah." Kylie swiped at her hair, drawing his attention to the scratches and abrasions that covered her already scarred palms.

"If we don't move and stay beneath the bushes—" she gestured to some undergrowth nearby "—maybe they'll move on."

He heard the desperate hope that filled her words. He hadn't heard any dogs and gave thanks to that. While he and Kylie might fool the men with their makeshift hiding place, they wouldn't be able to evade search dogs who could sniff out the faintest odor.

"If we stay hidden, there's a good possibility that they'll search a different area." His words were whispered, scarcely moving the air. They quickly took cover.

When a rustle of snow-covered ground came, and then another, this time closer, he put a finger to his lips.

Their pursuers were probably conducting a grid search. If they marked off this area, he and Kylie could breathe easy for a couple of hours. That would end when the men returned to check the area again.

The sounds grew fainter as their pursuers moved farther away.

"You're really calm," she noted.

"It's not the first time I've had to hide from the bad guys." He and his SEAL team had frequently played hide-and-seek with marauding groups of terrorists in the Stand. They'd become adept at hiding in the craggy rocks that had dotted the Afghanistan landscape, resting during the day when the heat was treacherous and moving at night when the temperature had cooled.

Worry had drawn lines on Kylie's forehead and in the small space between her brows. He longed to erase it, but there was no way around the fact that they were in a bad fix. He wouldn't get far if he tried to move; worse, he was getting weaker with every passing minute. But if they didn't move, they would be discovered.

He leaned toward her. "I need you to do something for me."

"Anything."

"I need you to get out of here before the men find us. Go and get help." Unspoken were the words *Save yourself.*

The mutinous look on her face told him what she thought of that. "No."

"It's the only way." He took her hand and cradled it in his own. "I can't make it."

"I won't leave you. Either we go together or we don't go at all."

He kept his exasperation out of his voice as he

asked, "What do you think will happen to you if we stay where we are?"

Tears streamed down her face. "I don't care."

He was powerless against her tears, and he knew it. "Okay. Suppose we both stay. How are we going to get out of here? I can't walk."

"You'll lean on me."

He let out a humorless laugh. "You can't carry me."

"I won't. I'll just be your crutch."

The idea of using Kylie as a crutch stuck in his craw. The events of late had made her fragile, both physically and emotionally. And he didn't want to slow her down when she was in very real danger.

A navy SEAL, ex or not, didn't lean on a woman, but that was exactly what he'd have to do.

After the men tracking them had cleared the area they were hiding in and had checked it off in their grid, Kylie and Josh ventured out. With him propped on her shoulder, she took an experimental step. And nearly crumpled under his weight. Okay. This was going to be harder than she'd thought.

She refused to give in and braced her shoulder under his arm for a second step. When she straightened, she felt her knees buckle. Though Josh carried not an ounce of fat on his body, he was a big man, probably outweighing her by a hundred pounds or more. She stiffened her knees and took a step forward.

"You could give a mule lessons in stubbornness."

"You comparing yourself to a mule?" She was trying to lighten the mood. They'd need every advantage they could have if they were to survive this, and a sliver of humor was all she had.

"Yeah. I guess I am."

"It fits."

"This isn't going to work," he said after a few minutes and pushed away from her.

"It has to. Now put your arm around my shoulders and let's try this again." This time, she knew what to expect and lifted with her legs.

They took a step forward. Another.

"We're getting it," she said after she felt they'd developed a rhythm of sorts. "We're getting it."

"But how long can you keep it up?"

She'd already asked herself the same question. Though she was in good physical condition, she couldn't support Josh indefinitely. Frustration and worry turned her voice tart. "As long as I need to," she said and gave him a fierce glare. "I'm not leaving you, so quit your whining and pick up the pace. Don't SEALs have some kind of thing about never giving up?"

"Something like that."

With Josh leaning heavily on her, their pace was slow, made even slower because of the treacherously slick ground. She watched every footstep, at the same time keeping an eye on Josh, making sure that he didn't slide.

His closeness caused her breathing to quicken and her heart to race.

She had never stopped caring about Josh, having carried his image in her heart ever since they'd parted. Though their circumstances were dire, his nearness infused her with sweet longing. How could she be entertaining such feelings when their lives were at stake? Yet she couldn't deny them. They had taken root and were growing stronger with every passing moment.

Get your mind in the game, girl. Her and Josh's lives depended upon her.

If this had been a movie, she would have waited anxiously to see how it unfolded. If it had been a book, she would have been turning the pages to get to the end. But it wasn't a movie. Nor was it a book.

It was her life. And, suddenly, the adventures she saw enacted in movies and described in books weren't exciting at all. She and Josh were being chased by bad guys with one goal: to get the flash card and then to kill them.

Her mind was as weary as her body, her thoughts jumbled into a tangled mess.

She and Josh picked their way over the ice-covered ground. She stumbled over a particularly uneven place but managed to right herself before she took Josh down with her. That would have been disastrous since she didn't know if she could get him back up. She didn't even know if she could get herself back up.

She should have concentrated on weightlifting during her workouts at the gym. The thought caused a small chuckle to escape her lips.

"What's so funny?" he asked.

"Just thinking that I should have done more weight training." She hoped he'd laugh along with her.

He didn't.

"You're wearing yourself out," he said after another twenty minutes had passed. "You can't keep carrying me." She heard the scowl in his voice.

"I'm hardly carrying you." She kept her voice low even though the men had moved far enough away that they couldn't hear her and Josh. Though she couldn't say for certain, she thought they'd moved to the west.

Josh was doing everything he could not to lean on her any more than possible, but she was taking more and more of his weight. "But a rest sounds good right about now."

They found a boulder to sit on, and Josh eased

himself down, allowing his injured leg to stretch out in front of him.

Her breath was coming in short pants that told their own story. She'd done her best to hide her exhaustion, but she knew she wasn't fooling him. She saw the concerned looks he darted her way when he thought she wasn't looking.

She undid her bag and brought out half of the remaining trail mix. They ate sparingly, knowing that it and a couple of power bars would have to last them until the next day. If their ordeal lasted more than that, they were in real trouble. After a small sip of water each, she repacked their things.

"We'd better get going," she said.

"No. *You'd* better get going." He held up a hand when she would have protested. "I've thought it through. You can't keep going like this."

"Who says I can't?" She did her best to infuse her voice with strength, but she wasn't fooling him. She could see it in his rock-hard gaze. "So what do we do?" she asked in a quieter voice.

"I spotted a place in the rocks. Over there." He pointed to a hollow in the ground about twenty yards in front of them. "I'll stay there. You go and get help. You'll move a lot faster without me. You can make it. Get to town and bring back help. That's the only way we'll survive."

"You can't stay here by yourself." If the men

hunting them found him, he wouldn't be able to defend himself.

"We don't have a choice."

"There's always a choice." With that, she stood, scanned the surroundings and found what she was looking for. She came back with two sturdy branches.

"You have your knife on you?"

He gave her a what-do-you-think look and pulled it from the sheath on his left ankle.

"Get busy and start taking the twigs off these branches." She didn't give him the opportunity to protest but started collecting smaller branches to use at the corners. "We're making a litter."

"Unless you plan on carrying two sets of poles at a time, it'll be a travois." He gave a small smile that told her he was joking.

She knew that. Right now, her brain was so splintered with worry that she could scarcely think. She knew that he was trying to take her mind off their situation with some humor.

Appreciating it, she made a face. "Okay, since you're so smart, what's the plural of travois?"

"You've got me there."

She wanted to tell him that everything would be okay, that they'd find their way out of this and have a story to tell their grandchildren.

That pulled her up short. *Grandchildren?* She and Josh were light years away from having a relationship, much less anything more permanent. That was aside from the reality that they might not make it out of here at all.

She couldn't afford the risk if she let down her walls for Josh. Parting from him eleven years ago had torn her heart into shreds. She wasn't ready to face that. Not again.

Obviously, her mind wasn't firing on all cylinders.

"What makes you think you can drag a travois over the ground any easier than carrying me?"

"I was hardly carrying you," she said. "I let you lean on me. But I think this will be better. Let me worry about pulling it."

Building a travois would require time and effort. Dragging it might leave a trail and even make sounds that could alert their attackers.

Mentally she cataloged the reasons why it didn't make sense and then balanced them with why staying together was the right call. Josh knew the way to Silveridge, the nearest town, approximately eight miles away. Having him with her made more sense than trying to find it on her own.

In the end, none of that mattered. She couldn't leave him. Period. She wouldn't abandon him.

"Take off your jacket," she told Josh.

He didn't waste time arguing with her, only did what she said. She did the same, then set about tearing the sleeves from their shirts. Removing even a layer of clothes in the extreme cold was dicey, but she needed the material if she was going to make a travois. In the end, she decided she didn't have a choice.

It was a rough-and-ready job, but it gave her what she needed. She used the sleeves bolstered with pine boughs to weave in and out to make the bed of the travois and tied them to the poles. It wasn't the sturdiest, but it would have to do.

When she put her jacket back on, she noticed the difference in warmth immediately. Even the thin material of her shirt's sleeves was better protection than nothing beneath her jacket. It couldn't be helped.

Between the two of them, they were able to fashion a decent enough travois.

She had one more chore to do, one she'd been putting off because she was afraid of what she'd find.

"Lie down," she ordered. "I need to look at your leg."

Once again he did as she instructed, but his scowl told her that he didn't like it.

Blood had soaked through the bandages. She needed to staunch its flow and then apply a fresh bandage. A check of their supplies showed that they were down to only a few bandages.

She removed the old bandage and tried not to

wince at the angry red wound. As quickly and efficiently as she could, she applied a new bandage and hoped Josh hadn't caught her gasp of dismay.

Though he hadn't said anything during the procedure, she understood that he knew just how bad his leg was.

"All ready," she said with as much cheer as she could summon.

She picked up the poles of the travois and gave an experimental tug. Okay. This was going to be harder than she had anticipated, but she could do it. She didn't have a choice. Somewhere she would find the strength to pull Josh to town.

After only a half hour into the trek, her shoulders burned as though a white-hot poker had been held to the flesh. Her arms weren't much better.

How could she keep going? Yet she couldn't stop. She had to get Josh to a hospital. His life depended upon it.

She paused for a moment, only a moment, but the relief was so tremendous that she stretched it into another. And another.

You can do this. The voice in her mind warred with the reality of her throbbing arms and shoulders. Her thigh muscles ached nearly as badly, as she'd used her legs to bear a good deal of the weight. Her breath whistled sharply from her overworked lungs while every muscle screamed in agony.

All it took was putting one foot in front of the other and then doing it again and again. What was with her? She'd been tired before. But she'd never pulled a travois with a two-hundred-pound man on it before.

Her breath was in rags, and her lungs stung as if they'd been filled with battery acid. Her vision blurred as a result. She blinked to clear it, to no avail.

She stopped to let the burning subside and found that her eyesight had cleared. A momentary blip, she assured herself. She'd make it to the next copse of trees and take a break.

A short break was all that she needed. Of course it was. Time for her muscles to relax, for her resolve to shift into gear once more.

"Kylie?"

So much for her hope that Josh would sleep through her pause.

"Problem?" he asked.

She wanted to laugh at the irony of the question. "No problem. Just getting my bearings."

"Keep heading s-south."

Grateful that she knew which direction was south, she nodded, forgetting he couldn't see her. "Will do."

His voice was slurred, she noted. Pain, certainly, but it was the worsening of the infection she feared the most. If the infection got into his bloodstream, things were going to get worse. Infinitely worse. With herculean effort, she pushed that from her mind.

For now, she had one goal: to make it to the next stand of trees. From there, she would make it to the one after that and then the one after that. Small goals added up to big achievements. She'd read that somewhere.

With that in her mind, she put one foot in front of the other and resumed trudging over the rough ground.

Do. Not. Give. Up.

The four words became her mantra. She matched her steps to them as they played in her mind. Make it to that bush. Make it to that pile of rocks. Make it to the next snowdrift. Just… make it. The self-imposed challenges kept her going until she no longer needed them; she only needed to keep lifting her feet and setting them down again.

You are stronger than you think. When she'd returned home from Afghanistan, she'd seen a therapist to deal with everything she'd undergone. The physical torture had been bad enough, but losing Ryan, her almost-fiancé, had been the worst.

She would never forget holding him as he bled out, begging him not to die and knowing that he was already gone. If he'd lived, if they'd returned to the States and gotten married as he'd wanted, where would she be now?

Not here. That was certain.

Was it guilt that she'd never given him the answer that he'd wanted that had caused the pain in her hands to continue? That was the therapist's diagnosis. Kylie had dismissed it, but it continued to niggle at her.

Had it taken seeing Josh injured and in pain for her to put the pieces together?

If so, what did that mean for her? For Josh?

The questions would have to wait. For right now, she had her hands full trying to save their lives.

If she'd believed in prayer, she'd have prayed. As it was, she could only hope she could do this. Hope was a paltry substitute for prayer, but it would have to do.

SEVEN

The first mile went okay. Sure, it was hard, but she was doing it. Sometime between the second and third mile, she started feeling the strain. Before the end of the third mile, she was limp with exhaustion and pain.

When she took another step, she wanted to weep, but tears weren't going to help so she gritted her teeth and took another step. And another.

They hadn't encountered their pursuers since they cleared the grid where she and Josh had been hiding. Were the men close by, ready to pounce at any moment?

Muscles burned across her shoulders, down her arms. Her back no longer screamed; it was the quiet agony that was somehow worse than the shrieking pain. Her mouth felt coated with sand, which made no sense as they were in the middle of a snow-covered wilderness. She tried to work up some saliva to allow her to swallow and get rid of the sand, but her lips and tongue were so dry that she couldn't even summon a drop or two of spit.

The coppery scent of blood was fresh in her nostrils. That made no sense either, and then she knew what it was. Her hands. The blisters she'd noticed earlier had probably popped.

Great. Just great.

Everything about her hurt, and now her hands were bleeding. The blood hadn't seeped through her gloves yet, but she could feel its moistness between her fingers. She did her best to ignore it. She had bigger things to worry about.

She ignored her hands, just as she ignored the fiery sensation in her shoulders and arms. She only wished she could ignore the fear that was somehow worse than any physical pain.

And then there was the cold. Exacerbated by their wet clothes, it had worked its way into their bodies with merciless persistence. With their nearly empty bellies, they had little energy. What strength they had was spent in fighting the cold.

So intent on her thoughts was she that she missed a fallen log and dragged the travois directly over it.

Josh's grunt caused her to set down the poles and hurry to him. "I'm sorry."

"Don't be," he said.

She knew he was angry, not at her but at himself. She wanted to erase the self-blame that filled his eyes, but she understood him well enough to know he wouldn't welcome comforting words, so she kept her mouth shut.

What was there to say? She couldn't tell him that things would get better. And she couldn't alert Josh to her concerns. He'd insist that she stop, that she leave him and make her way to town. The truth was, their circumstances were so bleak that even if she'd been able to rally the words, they would have stuck to her tongue.

Aside from that, she wouldn't fool Josh. He knew the score. She only wished the numbers would tip in their favor.

"Kylie. Stop."

The words came out more harshly than Josh had intended. Shouting at her was the last thing he wanted to do, but he had to get her attention.

He couldn't bear the thought of her pulling the travois another step. How she'd lasted this long, he didn't know. Though he couldn't see her, he could all but feel the strain on her body as she put one foot in front of the other with dogged determination.

She hadn't uttered a word of complaint. He wished he could summon the same resilience and unswerving resolve she showed, refusing to give up even when any rational individual would declare it was the right thing—the only thing—to do.

She kept going. Whether she didn't hear him or just didn't pay attention, he didn't know.

Physically, he felt better, having rested while Kylie pulled him. That, in turn, intensified his sense of guilt.

Her steps were becoming increasingly slow until they were more of a shuffle, her feet barely moving, only dragging over the ground in a sideways movement.

He tried again, this time gentling his voice. "Kylie, stop. Please." He breathed out a silent prayer that she would listen this time.

"Can't stop," she called over her shoulder. Unspoken were the words that if she stopped, she'd never be able to start again.

He understood.

He also understood that she was killing herself with the effort. The feisty girl he'd known had grown into a woman filled with grit who didn't let up, no matter what. He appreciated that quality; at the same time, he didn't want her to collapse because she was pushing herself too hard.

Because of him. Because he'd been careless enough to cut his leg on a nail.

Guilt sluiced over him in relentless waves that were as hard to bear as the growing pain in his leg. It didn't help that his brain felt fuzzy, his thinking foggy. "You're falling-down tired." Why did it sound like an accusation? He didn't mean it that way. Or maybe he did. He didn't know anymore. "You can't keep going," he added with as much patience as he could muster.

Her selflessness in pulling him on the travois and her determination not to give up only made him admire her more, stirring up old feelings. He tried to tell himself that they were only leftovers from the past, but that was a lie.

His feelings belonged to the here and now. Even while on the run and after a night spent roughing it, she was the most beautiful woman he'd ever seen. He wanted to share all that—and more—with her, but it wasn't the time or the place.

"Who says?" The umbrage in her voice would have caused him to smile another time. But not now. Not when she sounded like she was ready to keel over.

"At least take a rest."

"Can't."

The single syllable was more of a groan than a word. If he'd been able, he would have stood and forcibly taken the poles of the travois from her. From the jut of her chin, he knew he'd have a fight on his hands. Kylie had always been stubborn. It was that stubbornness that had kept her going, but even that couldn't defeat the sheer weariness she had to be feeling.

"Please," he said. "For me."

She paused, and he prayed that she was considering it.

He'd prayed more in the last thirty-six hours than he ever had. He knew God heard those prayers. It was no small blessing that the men hadn't caught up to them yet, but the obstacles hadn't let up. If anything, they'd grown. Now he was dealing with a heavy dose of guilt that only grew heavier with every step Kylie took. Not for the world would he have wanted her to be injured rather than himself, but he wished with all of his heart that it was he who was pulling the travois.

"Okay." The two syllables were a blend of reluctance and relief. "For a little while."

When she lowered the travois to the ground, he wanted to cheer. He'd gotten her to let go of the poles. Now all he had to do was keep her from picking them up again. She winced, and he twisted his head enough to witness the extreme care she took in removing her hands from the poles. What was going on?

And then he got it. Her hands were probably pocked with blisters from gripping the poles.

"Let me see your hands."

"They're fine."

"Take off your gloves."

"What if I don't want to?"

It was worse than he'd feared if she was so reluctant to remove her gloves.

He was angry. Angry at the men who were after them. Angry at Kylie. But mostly he was angry at himself. If he hadn't been so careless to cut his leg on a nail, they wouldn't be in this fix.

"I'm sorry," he muttered.

What did he do now? He could handle pain for himself, but knowing Kylie was in pain tore him apart.

He gentled his voice and tried again. "Kylie, please, take off your gloves. Let me see."

It wasn't a request but an order, however softly it was uttered. Normally, her hackles would have gone up at being issued such an edict, but she was so exhausted that she couldn't summon the energy to offer even a token protest.

Slowly, painfully, she removed one glove and then the other. Even those small movements hurt. Though the gloves had protected her hands for a while, the leather had worn through. Rubbed raw, with huge blisters forming on her palms, her hands were a mess. A few of the blisters had already popped and were now oozing pus and blood.

Just great. Josh wasn't the only one in danger of infection.

There was no way she could hide the damage from him. "I haven't had my manicure today."

He didn't laugh, and she feared that the joke

sounded as feeble to him as it did to her. Too bad. It was all she had. Reluctantly, she held out her hands, palms down.

Gently, he turned them over and growled. "Why didn't you say anything?"

"Because I knew what your reaction would be. It's not a big deal," she added. "They'll heal." In enough time. Right now, she feared infection might develop in the open wounds.

"Give me the first aid kit."

They'd used much of the supplies tending his leg; all that was left were alcohol cleansing pads and a few bandages. With infinite tenderness, he cleaned her palms.

The antiseptic stung, but she didn't flinch. When he wrapped her palms in gauze and then placed bandages over them, she steeled herself.

"We better look for a place we can bed down for the night," he said. "We aren't going any farther."

"You're really good at giving orders."

"Glad I'm good for something."

The bitterness in his voice was her undoing. "I've done everything I can. I don't know what else to do." She was beyond exhausted. Her arms and shoulders ached abominably. And her hands...

"Sorry," he said. "You've been a trouper."

Though she'd told herself they should keep

moving while it was still light out, she knew that neither she nor Josh were up to it. His breathing was short, labored, a testament to the pain he must be enduring.

Her own breathing wasn't much better. So much for her workouts at the gym.

It didn't help that another dust-up of snow was blurring the landscape. She started looking for a place they could take shelter. They both needed to get out of the snow and find a place where they could dry off and rest for a few hours. Just as deadly as their pursuers was the dropping temperature.

Her eyes passed over what looked like an indentation in a cliff, when something about it caused her to take a second look. It was a cave.

After checking it out to make sure an animal hadn't taken refuge there, she pulled in the travois. When she tried to help Josh out, he pushed her away. "Leave me," he said. "I'm too heavy for you to lift. I'll be comfortable enough here."

She undid the ties holding him in place, and he stretched. "You were amazing out there."

She didn't feel amazing. She felt like she was letting him down and letting herself down, too. Somehow, she'd grown to care for him again. Her heart gave a decided bump at the admission.

How had she allowed that to happen? When she'd gone to him for help, she'd warned herself against developing feelings for him. Fear for herself had sent her to him. Now it was fear for him, which was far stronger.

She pulled out two energy bars, then set hers aside, intending to give it to Josh. He needed it more than she did. When she judged the time right, she handed it to him.

"No," he said. "You're the one who's doing all the work. You should have both portions."

In the end, they both ate their own share. Though the energy bar tasted more like sawdust than actual food, she felt her energy picking up at having something in her stomach. She broke it off in small pieces, trying to stretch it out.

"Pretty rotten, isn't it?" he asked.

"Yeah. That's why I'm pretending it's a good old-fashioned candy bar loaded with real chocolate and sugar and nuts."

They finished the snack, and she found herself digging into the foil wrapping for any missed crumbs. She stuck the wrapper in her pack and wished she had a dozen more of the bars, bad tasting as they were.

Her belly no longer growled in hunger. Instead, there was a dull pain as though its walls were rubbing against each other, sloshed by stomach acids. The sensation brought back memories from the camp, where the guards had used starvation to keep the prisoners weak and unable to fight back.

"You're beautiful," Josh said unexpectedly.

Irritation brewed with pleasure to surge through her. The last thing she needed was Josh telling her that she was beautiful, not when she was feeling distinctly unbeautiful, not when she was wondering how she was going to go on.

"My hair is matted. I'm filthy. And I'm starting to stink. Then you go and say something like that."

Her voice rose with every word. She wanted to punch him. At the same time, she wanted to wrap her arms around him, hold him close and kiss him. She didn't think about her PTSD. She didn't think about the killers who were following them and could catch up with them at any moment.

"You'll always be beautiful to me."

She hadn't cried when her shoulders had burned pulling the travois. She hadn't cried when the blisters covering her hands had burst. But she cried now. Her shoulders shook with sobs that wouldn't stop.

Finally, the sobs subsided to give way to sniffles. When her hands started to ache, something they frequently did when she was feeling vulnerable, she rubbed them. She noted Josh's gaze in her direction, a question in his eyes.

"Want to tell me now how you got those scars?" he asked.

"It's an ugly story."

He only waited.

"The prison commandant wanted me to go on camera and denounce what the NGOs and our government were doing to help girls learn to read. I refused. So he cut my hands. Over and over."

She'd gotten the telling out without crying. That was progress, wasn't it? She hadn't been able to do that with the therapist.

Josh took her hands in his and gently caressed them, his fingers kneading the damaged flesh and bringing blessed relief. Such was his tenderness that the unwanted tears threatened to make an appearance again. "Thank you for telling me. It couldn't have been easy."

Feelings for him swirled through her mind, working their way to her heart. Hadn't she already lectured herself about falling for him again?

She pushed that away and focused on the now.

"No. It wasn't." But she was glad she had told him. His hands felt so good on hers that she didn't yank them away from his grasp as she might have. His touch brought back so many memories, the sweet memories of youth. At the same time, though, it stirred up new feelings, those of a woman. The woman she was today.

She looked at him and recalled the man she'd once loved and lost. She wanted to chalk up her emotions to the reaction of the danger they faced, but she knew that wasn't the truth. The truth was she was learning to care about the man far more than she'd ever cared about the boy.

Even with pain etching hard lines in his face, he was the most appealing man she'd ever known. His dark eyes, fringed by lashes most women would kill for, radiated an innate goodness that would never be dimmed.

He should have looked vulnerable now, but she could detect no vulnerability in him, only frustration that his body could not do what he wanted it to. Relying on someone else had always been anathema to him.

Some years back, she'd been on assignment in Germany. There, she'd visited a museum specializing in medieval art and had come across an oil painting of a soldier readying for battle, the leashed strength clearly visible in the set of his jaw and the bunched muscles of his chest and arms.

It had reminded her so much of Josh that she'd carried the image with her for years afterward.

"Penny for your thoughts," Josh said.

The quip brought her up short. She couldn't tell him what she was really thinking, so she brought their talk back to their escape.

"A penny would be a gross overpayment." She didn't follow up for several minutes, then asked,

"What are we going to do?" Absurd question. He didn't have answers any more than she did.

"We rest now," he said. "It'll be dark soon enough. Tomorrow morning, you're going to hike the rest of the way to town. When you get there, you're going to have your hands seen to and tell somebody where I am. It'll work out. You'll see." His voice was fading.

The weakness of it prompted her to remove her own coat and lay it over him. With only a shirt to protect her body from the cold, she shivered violently. In her worry for Josh, though, the shivering seemed of minor importance.

He was silent after that. His rough breathing told her he had fallen into an uneasy sleep. Despite what he'd said, she knew there was a very slim possibility of him surviving this. He was willing to sacrifice himself in order to give her the opportunity to live.

Though she no longer believed in prayer, she was tempted to beg the Lord for His help. Josh was right. She couldn't keep pulling the travois, but what choice did she have? Leaving him behind wasn't an option.

They had little in the way of supplies, especially food. She knew Josh would insist she take it with her so as to keep up her strength.

Was there a way out of this that didn't require Josh sacrificing himself?

What was it he had told her about answers to prayers? Something about the Lord answering prayers in His own way, in His own time.

The trouble was, time was running out for Josh. Time was running out for both of them.

She put a hand to his forehead, more concerned than ever when she found it hot to the touch. He was definitely feverish, and she had nothing to give him.

She listened. And listened some more. All she heard was the sough of the wind and the beat of her own heart. She lay on the hard ground and imagined herself nestled in a blanket in front of a roaring fire. *You survived six months in a prison camp*, she reminded herself. If she could endure that, she could do this. No problem.

At one time, she'd been a fervent believer in the Lord and His goodness. It was that faith that had sustained her when her parents had divorced and left her at age eighteen on her own. It was that faith that had spurred her to go to school and get her degree in journalism while working two jobs. It was that faith that had given her the courage to travel all over the world to capture images of the damage wreaked by hurricanes, tsunamis and war.

When she hadn't been able to attend church on her travels, she'd worshipped on her own, always giving thanks to the Creator.

After enduring the harshness in the prison camp and witnessing the inhumanity the guards had subjected the prisoners to—men and women and children alike—she had felt that faith, the one constant in her life, slip away until it had finally died altogether. Starvation, beatings and continual humiliations had whittled the faith from her until all that remained was a memory of the belief she'd once held so dear.

There'd be no relief in faith. Not for her. Not anymore.

She feared there'd be no relief from any quarter at all.

EIGHT

Josh groaned softly. Cold and pain had awakened him after only a few hours of sleep.

He hated the circumstances they found themselves in. He hated the cold. He hated the pain that was radiating in ever-increasing circles in his leg. Mostly, he hated his own helplessness.

He knew Kylie was hurting. He could barely bring himself to look at her, to see the lines of pain etched on her beautiful face, now covered with dirt and grit. Guilt and self-loathing were a cruel mix that lashed him with stinging stripes.

He had failed her badly. He had failed himself. *Quit feeling sorry for yourself.*

Too bad the words were easier said than done.

He thought of the SERE course he'd undergone before he had completed SEAL training and claimed his Trident: Survival. Evasion. Resistance. Escape.

Thanks to Kylie, they had both survived and evaded, but for how long could they keep it up?

At the moment, capture seemed imminent, and though both would do their best to resist, they had precious little reserves to call upon.

Face it. He couldn't crawl his way out of a paper bag right now.

"Don't," she said, startling him. He'd thought she was still asleep.

"Don't what?"

"Don't beat yourself up over what's happened. It wasn't your fault. None of it."

He'd been feeling sorry for himself, not a good look on anyone, especially not a navy SEAL.

He wanted to think further about their investigation but didn't have the energy. *Think about something else.*

"Tell me more about your time in Afghanistan," he said.

She was quiet for so long that he feared she wasn't going to answer. "Why do you want to know?"

"Because I care about you and want to understand what happened."

"Now isn't the time."

"Are you sure? Maybe it's exactly the right time." What he didn't say was that they might not have another time.

Her expression said that she understood too well. "Maybe you're right."

When she finally started, the words came out

in a frenzied rush, as though she had to get them out before she retreated into silence once more. "I accompanied an NGO that was working to establish a school for girls. And though I wasn't part of the NGO, I believed in their cause and wanted to show what was being done to help the girls receive an education."

Her smile came and went. "They were so eager to learn. They were like sponges, soaking up anything the teachers could give them. One of the workers wrote to his parents and asked if they could gather up books and send them. When a box of books arrived, the girls started to cry. They were that happy. A shipment of gold would not have been more welcome. One girl—she was only fourteen—she and I took a liking to each other. Her name was Nadime."

She raised her head to look at him. "Are you sure you want to hear this?"

He had a feeling he knew where this was going and wanted to tell her no, he'd changed his mind, but he forced himself to nod.

"The NGO workers and the village men had built a school. I was taking pictures that I sent back home. The girls were fascinated with the pictures and wanted to see everything."

He braced himself when pain filled her expression.

"When the soldiers came, I didn't understand

what was happening. Not at first. And then the shooting started." Her voice turned husky, as though her breath were caught in her throat, strangling her. "They killed all the villagers, except for the girls. They were going to be traded. They saved the NGO workers to be used as bargaining chips."

"And you?"

"And me." She took a long breath. When she continued, her voice was flat, as though every feeling had been sucked from it and from her. "They made us walk, for what seemed like days. The only food we were allowed was a cup of water and a little bit of rice at the end of the day. When we reached some kind of camp, they separated the men from the women.

"What they did…" He heard the grief in her voice, grief mixed with a good dose of fury. He understood. When grief couldn't contain all the horrors, fury took over. Oddly, the fury was easier to handle. Grief was another matter. It burrowed itself deep into the soul and heart.

"It's okay. You don't have to say it."

"The girls were traded with another group. The last time I saw Nadime, she was crying for her mother. I tried to reach her and was beaten for my efforts." Another long breath. "We were kept there for six months, until US forces came and rescued us. I heard that the girls were returned to their village, but all their parents had been killed. I think they were sent to a refugee camp." She closed her eyes, as though to blank out the dark memories.

His gut clenched, and his anger went on simmer as he imagined what Kylie had endured. No wonder she'd come out of the experience with PTSD. More than wanting to give into his anger, however, he ached inside at what she'd suffered.

He pictured her anguish at knowing that the girls she'd tried to protect were sent to a refugee camp. Much of the supplies sent to camps were confiscated by corrupt officials charged with distributing food, water, medical supplies and other necessities before they ever reached the people. They were sold on the black market. Worse than the corruption, though, was the violence, and even molestation, that went on with depressing regularity.

With all his being, Josh wished he'd been part of the rescue team. His hands fisted as he thought of what the commandant and guards of the prison camp where she'd been held had inflicted upon innocent civilians. Would he mete out the same treatment to them that they had shown Kylie and the others who had been starved and beaten all because they were trying to help girls whose only crime was wanting to learn to read? He wanted to think that he would show mercy, but he honestly didn't know.

"You're the most amazing woman I've ever known." The realization that old feelings were rekindling caused the breath to pinch tight in his chest. The woman she'd become was even stronger than the one he'd known eleven years ago.

"Hardly." She gave a dismissive gesture. "But I survived. And that's what we're going to do here. Survive." She uttered the last word so fiercely that he believed her. Almost.

"Thank you for telling me."

She dipped her head. "I haven't shared all of that with anyone, not even my therapist."

"Why not?"

"I don't know." Her expression turned thoughtful. "Maybe I just didn't want to say the words out loud."

That wasn't uncommon.

He wanted to tell Kylie that she needed to talk about all that had happened, but she didn't need him to tell her what to do. She just needed him to listen.

He longed to hold her, to comfort her, to do anything he could to wipe away the painful images. Did he dare to risk his heart if he were to take her in his arms and offer her comfort? He needed to protect her; at the same time, though, he needed to protect himself.

And so he did the only thing he could. He prayed.

* * *

Kylie was relieved when Josh closed his eyes again. The uneven rumble of his breathing told her he'd given in to sleep once more.

She didn't know how close the men chasing them were. They had probably holed up for the night, just as she and Josh had. Had they found a cave, as well? Or had they camped in the open?

Come daylight, they'd be on the hunt again. She and Josh couldn't outrace them. Nor could they outfight them.

She drifted. Or dreamed. She wasn't sure. Pictures unfolded in her mind, a slow-motion movie complete with captions. No, not captions… Instructions.

Startled by the vivid dream, she woke panicked, looked around and saw that Josh was where she'd left him.

Only the sound of his tortured breathing stirred the darkness.

The dream nagged at her. It had contained a niggle of an idea of how to save Josh and herself, but whatever it was had vanished. Could she recreate it? No. All she had left was the wisp of a memory.

She started with the facts.

Josh was unable to walk.

She was unable to pull him in the travois any farther.

The cold was worsening.

They had little food.

If they were to save themselves, it was up to her.

Ideas noodled around in her mind.

And then she had it. As each picture unfolded to reveal the next, she knew what she had to do. Rather than leaving Josh on his own and making the trip to town by herself, putting both of them at greater risk, she'd turn the tables. She'd go after the men chasing them.

She pushed the idea around in her mind. She didn't have many options. Did it make sense to go after the men herself? If she left Josh alone in the cave while she found her way to town, he'd be helpless. He was growing weaker by the moment. And what guarantee did she have that she'd make it to town?

After a mental tussle, she decided that it made sense. Though their pursuers hadn't found her and Josh yet, it was only a matter of time before they did. Better to go on the hunt and find them first. Surprise was a powerful element in taking down the enemy.

Granted, it was only a figment of a plan, but it could work. All she had to do was take out two or more bad guys and force them to help her get Josh to town. No problem.

A grin that was more of a grimace tugged at

her mouth. She could do this. She would do this. And she felt her energy return. More, she had her spunk back. It had been MIA for so long that she'd feared she'd never be able to count on herself again. Now she was ready to take the fight to the enemy.

Years ago, she'd had to face down several gang members in her quest to dig up a story. They'd done their best to intimidate her, but she'd stuck to her guns and gotten what she wanted.

What was the expression she'd heard from one of the SEALs who'd rescued her and the others in the prison camp? Oh, yes. *Ready, guns loaded and safeties off.* Could she imitate that SEAL, to ready herself, have her gun loaded and the safety off? The metaphor was close enough to the reality of the situation to have her lips press together in resolve.

She went through their meager supplies. A check of the pack revealed an extra pair of socks. She filled the socks with hefty rocks she found scattered around the cave, then tied them at the ends and gave one an experimental swing.

The rocks provided enough heft to give a good wallop. She would just have to get in the right position to give a good swing and make sure she hit her opponent where it would do the most good.

Not much. But she could work with it.

A mental tally of their weapons momentarily

deflated her enthusiasm. They had two guns between them. Fortunately, she was skilled in both weapons; however, the men after them were no doubt armed to the teeth with handguns and rifles. She couldn't leave Josh defenseless and would leave one weapon with him along with his knife. Though she lacked a man's strength, she had some first-rate moves courtesy of her martial arts training.

She set her teeth. "You can do this," she said quietly to herself. A scripture from Matthew that she'd memorized long ago came to mind. *With people this is impossible, but with God all things are possible.*

With that, she tidied her thoughts and did her best to sleep. She'd need all the energy and strength she could summon if she was to go up against two or more armed men.

She was going hunting.

NINE

Josh jerked awake, dismayed to find that he'd drifted into some kind of semiconsciousness without being aware of it. It took a moment for him to get his bearings, to realize that he was not on the outskirts of Kandahar fighting terrorists. He was in the Rocky Mountains battling home-grown killers who were every bit as dangerous.

Was this how it was to end? With him slipping in and out of reality until he finally gave way to the infection that was even now coursing through him?

When he'd been deployed, he and his buddies had occasionally engaged in dark speculations about the bullet that might take the life of any one of them. There were no certainties in combat. A bullet, he understood. But to be taken out by infection from a rusty nail wasn't how he'd pictured going out.

The maudlin trail of his thoughts scared him, and he did his best to force them from his mind. He was drifting now, his mind blank of thought.

He was both cold and hot, a strange paradox that confused him.

He tried to look around, but pinpricks of white blurred his vision.

Josh blinked. Another blink and his vision cleared.

Cold found its way into him, dug its claws deep and refused to let go. His body tried to shiver, but he found it couldn't. He lacked the energy to work up one good shiver. In other circumstances, he was certain he would have found that funny. In these, it wasn't funny at all.

Pain blossomed through him, radiating from his lower thigh, and even though he couldn't shiver, he could feel the pain just fine.

Josh heard Kylie make a trip outside and then return. She tossed back and forth as though her mind refused to settle. He understood. As exhausted as she had to be, she appeared unable to allow sleep to claim her.

Involuntarily, he let out a moan.

Kylie was by his side in an instant. "How are you?"

"Sore." He moved his head experimentally. "But better. I think." That was a lie. If anything, he was worse. He prayed the dim light concealed the sweat that had gathered above his lip and across his forehead. "What's on your mind?"

"I'm trying to work through something."

"Tell me."

With growing alarm, Josh listened to the plan Kylie outlined.

"No." He managed to refrain from shouting. "No way are you going after those men by yourself." He knew she must be feeling desperate to even suggest such a foolhardy idea. He didn't blame her; he was feeling pretty desperate himself.

"Do you have a better plan?" she asked in an even tone.

He didn't, but that wasn't the point. He wouldn't let her walk into the enemy camp. She couldn't take out two or more men. Not by herself. Even a trained operative like him might have trouble taking down heavily armed men.

Patience strained thin, he sent a hard look her way and then realized she wouldn't be able to see it. "They probably won't kill you, but they'll play with you. Make you hurt and hurt plenty before they take you to McCrane. Is that what you want?"

He immediately regretted his words. From what she'd told him about her time in the prison camp, she knew all about men "playing" with those they'd captured.

On the other hand, she might not make it as far as getting to McCrane. The men might just kill her on-site. Either scenario sent chills rattling through him.

She raised her chin, the movement catching his

gaze even though he couldn't make out her expression. "I'm doing this. With or without your help." She paused. "But I'd rather do it with you on my side."

He barked out a mirthless laugh. "What am I going to do? I can't even walk."

She made a noise that told him exactly what she thought of that. "You're going to tell me how to track them and then how to take them out. And I'm going to do exactly as you say. I'll bring them back here, and they'll help me get you to town."

"What'll we use for a vehicle?"

"Their truck."

Her plan wasn't just bad. It was terrible. How was she going to take out two or more men on her own? It didn't matter how trained she was in self-defense, she couldn't do it.

He wasn't ready to give in. He had to make her see that what she was planning was a suicide mission. As dire as their circumstances were, at least they were still alive. All he had to do was convince her to give up her foolhardy plan and to take off toward town.

He looked for a flaw in her plan. "I thought you said you wouldn't leave me," he pointed out.

"I'm not leaving you on your own." Her tone was one of infinite patience. "At least not for long," she amended. "Only long enough to take out the men and force them to help us."

Josh held his tongue and finally accepted that

he wouldn't talk her out of this. And, as she pointed out, what other choice did they have if she refused to leave him here? "If you're going to do this, you need to know some things."

She leaned in. "Tell me."

"Let's start with tracking." He held up his fingers, forgetting again that she couldn't see him. "Look for what doesn't belong. Anything. A scrap of paper. A tin can. Even a bent branch. No matter how careful they are, people leave something of themselves behind.

"And smell. Don't forget smell. Everyone starts to stink in the forest. That's nature's way of protecting them from predators like bears or mountain lions."

She made a face. "Don't remind me."

"I'm serious," he said. "You'll probably smell our trackers before you see them."

"Won't they smell me coming?"

"They aren't expecting you. Unlike animals, most people don't see or smell what they don't expect."

"What else should I look for?"

"Abandoned campfires. Depressions in the ground where someone was sleeping. Like I said, anything that doesn't belong."

"You know a lot about tracking."

"It's a lot of what I did when I was deployed. The landscape's different here, but the same rules apply. If you're really going to do this—"

"I am."

"Then don't try to take them out all together. You need to separate them. We know there are at least two of them. What we don't know is if there are any more. That'll complicate things."

Could he stand by and let her do this? And then he was reminded that he didn't have a choice in the matter.

Prayers swirled through his mind, quiet pleadings with the Lord for Kylie's protection. Prayer had become a constant companion while he was deployed; that hadn't changed when he'd returned and started work for the US Marshals and then S&J.

Eleven years ago, he hadn't been enough to keep her. Now, he feared he wasn't enough to keep her safe.

Kylie wanted to speed up time. Waiting to put her plan in action was taking a toll on her nerves. The adrenaline rush she'd experienced when she'd come up with the idea had settled to a low simmer. She wanted that rush. Needed that rush.

If she didn't leave soon, she feared she'd lose the momentum that had been pumping through her veins when the plan had first come to her. Who was she to think she could pull off such a plan? Sure, she'd had self-defense training, but she wasn't a pro. Not by any means.

Josh must be secretly laughing at her.

"Right along now, you're wondering if you can do it, aren't you?" Josh asked.

"Something like that." Oh, how she hated to admit it. Hated to acknowledge that she had a boatload of doubts, along with an equal number of fears, that hadn't occurred to her when she'd first conceived of the plan.

"Did you ever doubt yourself when you were in the SEALs?" she asked.

"Not before we executed a plan, no. It was only after it was over that I thought I ought to have my head examined and wondered how my team and I managed to get out alive. There was this one time…" He stopped, shook his head.

She looked at him in amazement. "I'm having a hard time believing that you were ever afraid."

"Believe it. SEALs have giant egos, but in the end, we're just human, like everyone else. It's natural to have doubts, but you can do this."

"You didn't think so earlier," she pointed out.

"I had some doubts," he admitted, "but I hear the resolve in your voice. You're determined. That counts for a lot."

Warmth washed through her at the words. "Thanks. I needed to hear that." If he believed she could pull this off, then she knew she could.

"Don't thank me."

For six months after returning to the States, she'd seen a therapist. She'd wept, cried and finally demanded to know why she wasn't getting back to her normal self.

"You went through a terrible ordeal," the therapist had reminded her. "You can't just snap your fingers and make those memories disappear. Give yourself time to recover, to grieve over the friends you lost.

"You're stronger than you think," he had said during their last session. "Never forget that."

The words had remained with her, a source of comfort and a reminder that she had not only endured the ordeal, she had survived.

She called upon that now as she helped Josh move farther into the cave in case their pursuers got past her.

"You don't have to do this," he said. "We'll find another way."

There wasn't another way, and they both knew it.

She wanted to tell him that she had never stopped caring about him, but she kept the words to herself. Another time, another place. Maybe. For now, she had to focus on finding the men intent on killing them and then forcing them to help her get Josh to help.

Mentally, she prepared herself. She wouldn't kill them. Not unless absolutely necessary, but she would if it meant saving Josh's life and her own. If her time in the prison camp had taught her anything, it was that squeamishness had no part in survival.

Those who had managed to stay alive after enduring the brutal treatment their captors had inflicted upon them hadn't done so by turning away from what had to be done. They had done what was necessary, just as she would do now.

"Like I said," Josh continued, "do your best to separate them. I'm figuring there are two, maybe three, men on our trail. Take them out one at a time."

"What if I can't?"

"Watch. Bide your time, then be prepared to strike when the time is right. You'll know."

She listened.

"Take care of yourself," he said. "I haven't lost a client yet."

"Is that what I am? A client?"

He looked uncomfortable. "Friend."

Friend sounded right. So why did she want more? With more effort than it should have taken, she pushed that from her mind.

"It's time," she said.

Fear rushed through her at what she was planning. Overriding the fear, though, was a cold determination. The will to survive. No one would take that from her. No one could.

With that, she prepared for war.

TEN

Josh despised being left behind. He'd have rather taken a bullet than send Kylie off on her own. No soldier, no real soldier, rested easy if he was forced to sit by and watch as others fought his battles.

His gaze followed Kylie as she climbed out of the cave, her bag hampering her movements. How she'd managed to get him in there in the first place was still a mystery. She must have used every ounce of strength she had to pull the travois through the small opening.

He hadn't let on how bad off he was. There was no sense in worrying her more than she was already.

His leg no longer hurt. That was good. Right?

But he was burning up. Not good.

If he had been physically able, he would have stopped Kylie from going on this mission. The irony of it wasn't lost on him. If he'd been physically able, they wouldn't be in the situation in the first place.

He'd wanted to tell her before she left that he was gut-busting proud of her, but all he'd managed to get out was a grunt. Did she understand how much he admired her and yet how afraid he was for her? The warring emotions tore through him, a tornado of respect and frustration, love and anger. The anger was self-directed, that he couldn't do anything to stop her and didn't see any other way out for them.

If she'd agreed to head out on her own, she might have made it to town. If she didn't come back from her self-imposed mission, he would never forgive himself.

In the quiet, where the only sound was that of his labored breathing, he prayed. Prayed for Kylie. Prayed for himself.

Senses on high alert, he listened with his whole body. Was that a rustle in the bushes? Had the men gotten by her and were even now planning their attack on him?

Had they taken her captive? If so, what were they doing with her? To her? Worrying held its own kind of terror. What if she was even now being interrogated? What if…

Images crowded his mind, and he did his best to dispel them. Entertaining gruesome pictures wouldn't help.

But he couldn't stop the questions racing through his mind. How could he have allowed the woman he had never stopped loving to track potential killers *on her own*? He'd dated sporadically over the last eleven years, but none of the women had ever touched his heart. They had been pleasant enough companions, but that was all. There'd been no connection with them. Finally, much to his mother's chagrin, he'd given up dating altogether.

If he was honest, he'd have admitted years ago that there had never been anyone for him but Kylie. Never had been, never would be.

The tears she'd shed earlier had sliced his heart into tiny pieces. Not for the first time, he wondered how people could treat their fellow human beings in ways that defied description. He thought he'd seen the worst the world had to offer and knew he had only been fooling himself. Pain and cruelty knew no bounds.

That Kylie had survived what she'd endured spoke volumes about her strength and courage. That she had come out on the other side, ready to take on new enemies and fight for what was right, only added to the weight of the remarkable woman that she was.

She was remarkable. Why hadn't he told her that before she'd left, encouraged her? She'd needed that more than she had the few things he'd been able to tell her about taking down the men pursuing them. Was it because he was ashamed that he couldn't go with her?

The answer came swiftly. Yes.

She was strong, fit and able, but she was still a woman pitted against two or more killers. He had given her what advice he could in tracking and capturing her quarry. But was it enough? She'd had nothing to eat in over twelve hours and precious little rest.

If she managed to track the men, if there were only two men rather than three, if she was able to separate them and if she could take them out... There were too many *ifs*. He was burning up again. *Ifs* were a part of his work, but Kylie shouldn't have to face them, not alone. His vision clouded. *Ifs* got people killed. *Ifs*...

The darkness took him before he finished the thought.

Kylie knew Josh had tried to hide how sick he was, but she'd seen the unhealthy color in his face, had smelled the foul sweat that came from fever. She had to do this. What was the motto? Failure was not an option.

If she wasn't able to get him to a doctor soon...

Following his tips, she tracked the men in less than an hour. Finding them wasn't difficult. They'd taken no precautions in covering their tracks, clearly not concerned that the hunted would turn hunter.

That part had been relatively easy. Now came the hard part.

They'd spent some time building a snow wall to protect them from the worst of the wind. She had to give them props for that, but they'd flubbed every other rule of wilderness tracking, including building a fire that gave away their location from a good distance. She didn't blame them for wanting the warmth, but the scent of woodsmoke was as good as a neon sign signaling their location.

She counted three men. Okay, that wasn't exactly good news, but she refused to let it throw her. With Josh's words fresh in her mind, she speculated on how to separate the men and cull one from the other two.

How to separate them? When she saw one man leave the campfire and head into the thicker woods, she had her answer.

Distract him when he was returning from answering nature's call. She fingered the chain at her neck, a gift from Josh shortly before they parted eleven years ago. She'd kept it as a reminder of that long-ago summer. Now she held on to it for a lingering moment.

For courage.

For strength.

For victory.

Okay. She could do this.

When she heard him making his way back to the camp, she nestled at the side of a tree and gave a faint moan. From her vantage point, she could see his hesitation as he retraced his steps after taking care of business.

Another moan on her part, more plaintive this time.

"Who's out there?" he called. "Bert? Vinnie?"

She let a third moan answer for her.

"Bert, if that's you playing with me, I'm gonna—" His threat went unfinished as he thrashed through the snow-covered ground with no regard for the racket he was making.

She smiled to herself. He was angry now. Angry and careless. A dangerous combination for him, but a plus for her.

When he was close enough, she made her move and leaped from her hiding place. When he came close, she swung the rock-filled sock at the back of his head. He dropped with a thud. Exhilaration coursed through her. She'd done it. One down, two to go.

The man's partners didn't show up. Had they heard him fall? Or were they just playing it safe? She tied him up with a zip tie she'd gotten from Josh.

She took one of his gloves and stuffed it in his mouth. It wouldn't do to let him cry out to his compatriots. Finally, she removed his boots and bound his ankles with another zip tie. The boots she tossed to the side.

Carrying him was out of the question, so she rolled him into the underbrush to conceal him and then did her best to cover their tracks in the snow.

She didn't deceive herself into believing it would be as easy to take out the other two men. When this one didn't return within a reasonable time, they'd be on their guard and would start looking, not just for their buddy but for whoever had taken him out.

Preparation was key, and she started with making certain her weapon was secured in her waistband.

The other men hadn't grown alarmed yet. She'd give them a few more minutes before they started searching. She edged closer to their camp and listened.

"Where's Bob?" one man asked. "It shouldn't take him this long."

"Don't know. Maybe he got lost." The other man, the smaller of the two, snickered.

"How far did he have to go?" The question was clearly rhetorical. She listened as the bigger man, whose face resembled a hunk of unpolished granite, appeared to give orders. "Why didn't you keep an eye on him?" he asked, irritation plain in his words. "You know he's a loose cannon."

The smaller man grumbled, "Since when did I become his babysitter?"

"I didn't say that." Annoyance coated every syllable.

Clearly the men were growing on each other's nerves. Could she use that to her advantage?

"Go check on him," the big man said. "If he's gotten himself lost, we need to find him. We can't afford to have him stumbling around and giving away our location."

"Why don't you go look for him?"

"Look, Vinnie. I'm the boss of this outfit. You do what I say when I say it."

The one named Vinnie raised his fist, then slowly dropped it. "Someday you'll push me too far, Bert."

She approached from the south and came up behind the smaller of the two men. Better to take him on first.

As silently as possible, she closed the distance between them and, when she was less than a foot away, pulled her gun and held it to Vinnie's back. "Drop your weapon and kick it away."

A sharp hiss of breath told her that she'd succeeded in taking him by surprise. He did as she'd instructed, kicking his gun into some nearby bushes.

"Now you," she said to the other man as he

approached. "Take out your weapon and kick it away."

Bert glanced at Vinnie, held at gunpoint, and begrudgingly did as she said.

With both men disarmed, she thought of her next move.

"Get over there by your partner," she ordered Bert.

It was safer to have the two men close together rather than spread out. Bert did as he was told, but he had his own surprise and pulled a second weapon from the back of his waistband. "Now you drop *your* weapon," he told her.

The two of them faced off. If she dropped her gun, he would probably kill her. She was reminded of old Westerns where the good guy squared off from the bad one.

"I'm figuring you ain't as good with a gun as I am," Bert said, "and I can fire off a bullet faster than you can blink."

He was right, of course.

"I won't kill you. That's not what we were paid to do. Killing costs extra."

With little choice, Kylie dropped her weapon.

"Tie her up," Bert ordered Vinnie. "And while you're at it, stuff something in her mouth."

After retrieving his gun, Vinnie started to do as ordered, then abruptly stopped and pointed it at Bert. "You do it. I'm tired of taking orders from you."

Bert looked stunned at this show of rebellion and reached to grab the weapon from the other man. In the scuffle, Bert dropped his own weapon. While the two men wrestled for Vinnie's gun, it went off. Vinnie dropped to the ground. The slack look on his face and the spreading crimson stain on his chest told their own story.

Kylie couldn't afford to feel any regret. She snatched up her weapon and aimed it at Bert before he could train a gun on her. She needed only one man to pull the travois.

Not a sign of remorse crossed Bert's face at the other man's death.

Still holding the gun on him, she pulled a zip tie from her pocket and handed the restraint to him. "Tie this around your wrists. Make sure you pull it tight. Once we get back to where I left my friend, you're going to help me take him to your truck."

He sneered. "You gonna make me?"

"Try me."

He did as she ordered, but the look in his eyes promised that this wasn't over. With Bert in the lead, a gun to his back, and her giving directions, they started back to where she'd left Josh.

When Bert suddenly spun and lashed out with his leg, she was ready. She sidestepped his kick, then cuffed him at the side of the head with her cupped palm. She'd picked up the move in her Krav Maga training, a good one if you wanted to get a foe's attention but not knock him out completely.

He staggered a bit but remained standing.

"You try that again and I'll use this—" she gestured with her weapon "—rather than my hand. Got it?"

"Got it." He glared at her, meanness glittering in his eyes.

If she hadn't been so intent on getting back to where she'd left Josh, she might have been concerned by the naked hatred she read in his gaze. As it was, though, he was no more than an annoyance. She had more important things on her mind than worrying about a man who was clearly a bully.

They made their way back to where she'd left Josh. By the time they reached the cave, dawn had come and gone, but there was no breathtaking sunrise to lift her spirits. There was only a dirty smear of light that reflected her mood.

She forced Bert into the cave. "Look who I found," she said to Josh.

A half smile found its way across his face. "You did it."

"Thanks to your tips." As she looked at him more carefully, she saw that it wasn't really a smile at all, but a twist of his lips that couldn't hide the pain. It only added to her urgency to get him to a hospital.

"Bert here volunteered to help us get you to his truck."

When Josh raised his brow at the word *volunteered*, she smiled, hoping to cheer him up a little at the humor in it. "Well, maybe he didn't exactly volunteer. And then he's loaning us the truck to drive to town. What's more, he insisted we have these." She poured out the candy and jerky. Concerned Josh wasn't strong enough to manage on his own, she unwrapped the snacks and held up a chocolate bar to his lips while keeping her gun trained on Bert. She was gratified when Josh took a couple of bites.

"Try some jerky," she said and handed him a piece of the dried meat. He needed the protein.

Josh took a bite of jerky before putting it down as though it took too much effort to eat. His lack of appetite was almost as concerning as the sickly color of his face. Had it only been yesterday that they were desperate for food?

Kylie had been riding an adrenaline high, but the rush she'd experienced only a short while ago when she'd captured the men had rapidly vanished upon realizing that Josh was too weak to even eat.

She considered tying Bert's wrists to the poles

but rejected the idea. He needed to be able to lift the poles and maneuver them.

With some difficulty, they got Josh, still lying on the travois, out of the cave. She winced with every twist and turn, knowing that each jolt sent daggers of pain through him.

"You can't make me pull this thing," Bert growled once they'd cleared the cave.

She trained her gun on him.

"Oh, I think I can. But if you refuse, you'll be doing it with a bullet in you."

"You'd shoot me? I don't think so." He sounded smugly sure of himself.

She didn't hesitate and shot him in the upper arm, making sure she only grazed the fleshy part. She didn't want to disable him; she still needed him.

A howl ripped from the man's lips. "You shot me!" The disbelief in his voice should have been satisfying, but she was too worried over Josh to appreciate it.

"I warned you. Now pick up your feet and get moving. Remember that I'm right behind you. If you stop, if you complain, if you do anything I don't like, I'll shoot you again." She meant it. She didn't have time for anything other than getting Josh the help he needed.

"You'll pay for this," Bert said.

"I was hoping you'd say that. It gives me a reason to shoot your other arm if you do anything I don't tell you to."

He muttered under his breath. Fortunately for him, she couldn't make out what it was.

The first leg of the journey went smoothly enough until Bert started to lag and she had to motivate him by aiming her gun at his other arm. She didn't blame him. He had nothing to look forward to now but serious jail time.

They made an awkward procession, but it worked. Bert issued more threats, but there was no real heat behind them. He knew he was beaten. By the time they reached the truck, he was panting heavily. The truck had been parked away from the men's camp where the trees were thinner.

"Help him in the truck," she said.

Bert undid the straps holding Josh to the travois and lifted him into the passenger seat.

"Fasten the seat belt around him," she instructed.

With another spate of muttering, Bert did as ordered.

Once Josh was settled, she considered what to do with Bert. She didn't want to leave him unguarded, but she couldn't take him with her and Josh. Even bound, he might be able to overpower her while she was driving.

She fastened a zip tie around Bert's wrists,

then motioned to him to sit down. She knelt beside him and removed his boots.

He wouldn't be going far. Not in this cold and not without shoes.

"You can't leave me here," he whined.

"Watch me." She gathered up his boots and carried them to the truck.

Josh roused a bit. "You're something else," he said when she got behind the wheel.

"I'm practical." She slanted him a worried look. "How are you feeling?"

"Better now." He barely got the words out before lapsing into unconsciousness again.

She told herself she'd done a good job. She'd captured the men after her and Josh. More importantly, she had transportation to get him to the hospital, but none of that mattered if she lost him.

Another look at his drawn face had her concern for him deepening. His skin was the color of old-fashioned school paste.

The sooner she got him to the hospital, the better. She started the engine and pulled away, noting the murderous look on Bert's face as she passed. She and Josh rode in silence. That was okay with her. If they talked, she might not be able to keep her worry to herself.

When they reached a main road, she noted that snow had been pushed to the side by repeated traffic. Despite that, slick spots still dotted the surface. As the clouds obscured the sun and the temperature dropped, she had to slow down, afraid she'd hit a spot of black ice.

Another glance at Josh told her that he was fading. He slumped further in the seat until only the seat belt was holding him in place.

"Josh?"

He didn't respond.

Time was running out.

The road had narrowed to a stingy two lanes. In addition, the snow had started up again. She wondered if she should be grateful for its steady fall that kept her attention on the road and prevented her attention from drifting to Josh.

She pressed down on the accelerator.

Hurry.

ELEVEN

Kylie struggled to focus. Worry, edged with a large dose of leftover adrenaline courtesy of taking down the trio of men, charged her senses.

Josh hadn't spoken since they'd started on their way. She wanted to believe he was only sleeping, but this wasn't a healthy kind of sleep. He appeared to have slipped into unconsciousness. His breathing was shallow, punctuated with a shuddering cough.

Unexpectedly, she found herself thinking of the words of a childhood prayer, something she hadn't done in a very long time.

She drove as fast as she reasonably could, but the grayish light and patches of black ice forced her to slow her speed. Sliding off the road wouldn't help.

She followed signs with a large *H*, indicating the hospital. When she drove to the emergency entrance, she honked, waiting for help. She took off her glove and put her hand to Josh's forehead.

His skin was clammy to the touch, and his face, usually deeply tanned, was a putrid green.

"Hold on just a little longer," she whispered.

"He cut his leg on a nail," she told the two orderlies who transferred him from the truck to a gurney and wheeled him into the ER. "I'm pretty sure infection has set in." She was running along beside them, fully intending to stay with him, even knowing that was impossible.

"Let us see to him," one snapped when she attempted to barge her way through double doors that prohibited entrance to anyone but hospital employees.

"The best thing you can do is stay out of the way," the other said with more compassion.

She slumped against the wall.

While Josh was being examined, her hands were seen to by an ER doctor who gave a low whistle. "What did you do to them?"

Unwilling to go into the whole story, she only shook her head and waited while he treated them. Though she longed to find a place where she could clean up, she couldn't leave without news of Josh's condition. Doing her best to ignore the looks people directed at her, she staked out a place in the waiting room. The smell of disinfectant stung her nostrils, but it was the fear oozing from the people anxiously awaiting news about loved ones that overpowered everything.

She understood. Too well.

Fear had its own odor, one that seeped into the pores. She needed a shower in the worst way, but even that wouldn't wash away the stink that clung to her.

She supposed she should call the authorities and tell them of the men she'd left in the woods. They were probably freezing. Though they didn't deserve any consideration, she didn't want to have their deaths on her conscience. After getting the state police on a hospital phone, she explained that she and her friend had been attacked in the woods and managed to get away. She then gave the location of the men and promised she'd make herself available for a statement the next day.

When a nurse walked into the waiting room, everyone stood, Kylie included. The nurse found the appropriate people and delivered news about a patient. Kylie approached him and asked about Josh.

"Your friend's in surgery. Go home," he advised. "When we learn something, we'll let you know."

"I can't leave. Not until I know he's going to be all right."

Eyes warm with sympathy, he said, "You look like you're about to fall over. Your friend isn't the only one who needs some rest."

She supposed she did look the worse for wear.

"Like I said, go home. You can't do anything

for your friend here. Do we have your contact information?"

Kylie started to mumble an answer and realized she didn't know what to say. What would the nurse say if she told him that she couldn't go home because she was afraid it was being watched and that she'd ditched her phone because she was being chased by men intent on killing her? Beyond that, she didn't have enough money on her to rent a motel room, even a cheap one.

The nurse gave Kylie a sympathetic look. "We have a couple of rooms here for family members with no place to go. I think there's one empty if you'd like me to arrange it for you."

"Th-that would be won-wonderful." In her gratitude, Kylie tripped over her words.

A shower and shampoo later, and donned in pink scrubs that the nurse had brought her, Kylie lay down on the narrow cot, intending to close her eyes for only a few minutes. When she awoke, the room was dark. How long had she slept?

Was Josh any better?

Feeling more than a little self-conscious in the scrubs, she found out what room he was in. After explaining to the floor nurse that she was the one who had brought Josh in, she was given grudging permission to see him, but for only two minutes.

He looked pale in the lights of the room that had been dimmed for the night.

When the doctor she'd spoken with earlier appeared, he gave Kylie a stern look, then smiled slightly. "Your friend is doing remarkably well. His vitals are normal. Everything looks good." He looked over her scrubs, and his smile broadened. "I can see that one of our nurses set you up."

She nodded.

"You got him here just in time," the doctor said, his voice grave once more. "A few more hours and it would have been too late to stop the infection. He might have lost the leg." He glanced at her bandaged hands. "I'm glad to see you got those attended to."

She scarcely heard him. "Please tell me that Josh is going to be okay."

"He'll be fine. Given some rest and time, he'll be good as new."

She could only imagine how the idea of rest and time was going to go over with him. They'd deal with that when it happened. Right now, it was enough to know that he was being cared for.

In the meantime, she had to keep him safe.

The truck she'd taken would be easily identifiable, and that meant it could be traced. Once McCrane and Winslaw discovered that their men were behind bars, they'd hire more to come after her and Josh.

They weren't safe and wouldn't be safe as long

as she had the flash card in her possession. And when she handed it off to the right person? What then?

She feared they'd never be safe again.

Josh dreamed.

Only the dreams were more the stuff of nightmares.

He and Kylie being pursued through the wilderness by men intent on killing him and abducting her. The crippling pain in his leg. Fear for Kylie as she set off on her own to take out the hostiles.

He shook off the remnants of the nightmare and focused on the present.

A day and a half had passed since he'd been admitted to the hospital. He was feeling better today and anxious to talk, but what did you say to the person who saved your life despite him doing everything he could to discourage her?

A smile touched his lips as he recalled how she'd forced one of their pursuers to carry him on the travois to their truck and then left him there in the wilderness. His smile did a belly flop when he thought of how he'd let her down.

She was stubborn and strong and tough and, above all, loyal. She hadn't given up on getting him to the hospital. Since he'd been in the hospital, they hadn't done much talking. He'd slept for much of the time while she'd sat by his bed, a fierce protector.

Guilt piled on his shoulders along with a dawning awareness that he and Kylie weren't safe here. When McCrane didn't hear back from his men, he'd start looking. If the men had been taken into custody and any one of them had asked for a lawyer, word would have made it back to the boss.

All it would take was for just one of the men to have told McCrane's lawyer that Josh was badly injured and needed medical care to have teams scouring the hospitals, looking for him and Kylie.

McCrane and Winslaw wouldn't give up searching for them. One thing he'd learned during his work was that bad guys were all the same. Their nationalities, their skin color, their ideologies might be different, but at the core, they all wanted one thing: to control others.

He and Kylie needed protection.

He pressed a call button. When a nurse arrived, he told her that he needed a phone.

Within a few minutes, he was talking with his S&J associate Luca Brady.

Josh outlined the situation as he would a sitrep.

The ex-ranger's response to the situation report was equally terse. "Be there at 1300."

Kylie didn't like the look of the men who had just entered the waiting room. Nor did she like the expression in their eyes, one of cold resolve. Though she didn't recognize them as any of the men who had chased her and Josh, they had the same look about them: tough and mean.

She slipped behind a large plant and listened when they talked with the receptionist at the front desk, worry ribboning through her. When she heard them ask about a "friend" who might have been brought into the hospital with a leg injury, she hurried to Josh's room.

She knew the hospital wouldn't give out information about patients, but she also knew that men like that wouldn't let that small obstacle stop them.

"We have to get out of here," she said upon walking into Josh's room, and then told him about the men she'd seen in the waiting room.

"I called Luca. He'll be here in ten minutes."

She feared they didn't have two minutes, much less ten.

When she saw the two men walking purposefully down the hallway, she knew she and Josh were in trouble. Their guns had been taken when she'd checked Josh into the hospital. She looked wildly about the room, looking for anything she could use as a weapon.

A stainless steel bedpan. A bottle of cotton swabs. A pitcher of water.

Think.

Her gaze landed on a small locker where she assumed Josh's belongings were stored. Though the pants had probably been thrown away, maybe his belt had been kept. She found the belt and wrapped it around her fist, making certain that the buckle was facing outward.

When the first man entered the room, she was ready and plowed her fist into his jaw with all her might. He grunted in pain as the metal buckle bit into his skin.

She didn't let up and kept grinding the buckle into his face until he flung her away. She landed on the linoleum floor but sprang up immediately, ready to do battle again.

Josh ripped the IV from his arm, took the pole and slammed it into the gut of the second guy. In his weakened state, however, he lacked strength, and his opponent grabbed the pole from him and threw it to the ground.

Just when Kylie was ready to jump on him, a third man barged in. She was about to use the bedpan on him when he caught her wrist. "Hold on. I'm on your side."

Luca. Now that she wasn't in the midst of battle, she recognized him. Luca threw his weight behind a punch that had Josh's attacker dropping to the ground. He tied up both men using zip ties.

By this time, bystanders had gathered in the hallway.

"Looks like the SEALs needed the Rangers to pull their fat out of the fire," he said.

Josh snorted. "Get us out of here."

Kylie was worried for Josh. He wasn't well enough to leave the hospital, but what choice did they have? "How are we getting out of here?" she asked.

"Find us a wheelchair," Luca said.

She left the room, ignoring the group that was dissipating outside the door, found a wheelchair and took it back to the room.

Josh climbed into the chair. "Let's roll."

Once they got outside and into the vehicle, Luca drove west of town, taking them to a small bungalow.

Its unassuming appearance caused Kylie to wonder if it was safe.

"Don't let its looks fool you. It's fortified on the inside and the outside," Luca said, apparently guessing at her thoughts. "No one's getting in there unless they have an RPG. You'll be safe enough here. What's more, it isn't on the books."

"Did you get the boss's okay?" Josh asked.

Luca gave a quick nod. "You know Gideon. He'd do anything for his people. By the way, that guy you tangled with at the gas station didn't give up anything. Far as I can tell, he didn't have anything to give up."

"Tell Gideon thanks for me."

"Call me if you need something." Luca turned to Kylie. "See that he gets some rest."

Kylie nodded. "Thank you. For everything."

"Josh is one of ours," Luca said simply. He handed her two sets of keys. "Two of our guys parked a couple of trucks in the garage."

Kylie had more reason than ever to appreciate Luca when she saw the sacks of clothes plus burner phones for her and Josh. She couldn't wait to shed the hospital scrubs and get into some real clothes.

Josh took a sack of clothes and disappeared into one of the bedrooms.

"Luca came through for us again," he said when he reemerged a few minutes later in jeans and a flannel shirt. He slipped one of the guns his friend had left into his waistband. "He's as good as they come. He saved my team more than once when we were deployed in the Stand at the same time as his Ranger unit."

She knew that those who had served in the Middle East often referred to Afghanistan as the Stand.

"It's a good thing he's on our side," Josh added. "Once, he held off six tangos while another buddy and I got our wounded from a courtyard where they'd taken fire. He refused to give up, even when it seemed we wouldn't make it. He ended up taking two bullets that day."

"Then I'm doubly glad he's on our side." She gave Josh a critical study. "You're looking better."

"I'm sorry. Sorry for not believing in you. And I'm sorry to have caused that." He gestured to her bandaged hands.

"They'll heal. The important thing is that you're going to be all right."

"The doctor said I'd be good as new."

To her mortification, tears appeared in her eyes. She'd been afraid—so afraid—that Josh would die, all because of her. She didn't think she could have lived with it. For the first time in days, she felt like they might be okay.

Did he know how she felt about him? She longed to tell him, but they were still in the midst of a very real danger, one that wouldn't let up until they figured out what the bad guys were up to and brought them to justice. But what if he didn't accept her feelings for what they were... Would he dismiss them as gratitude on her part?

"It's okay," she said, swiping at her cheeks as the tears fell. "I'm just glad you're going to be all right." She studied him another moment, the man who'd nearly lost his life to keep her safe, and before she knew what she was doing, she leaned in and pressed her lips to his.

Feeling after feeling poured through her as she kissed him. Wrapped up in the sensations, she let her mouth linger there for longer than she'd planned.

Then, acutely aware of what she'd done, she pulled back. A sharp pang washed through her at the loss of contact. What had she been thinking?

"This isn't smart," she said. "We have things to do."

"No." His soft voice sounded flat. "It isn't."

She nodded. This was what she wanted, wasn't it? For him to agree with her? Then why did she wish with all her heart that he hadn't?

Josh wanted to prolong the kiss.

He wanted to take their relationship back to where it had been eleven years ago. No, that wasn't true. Then, he'd been scarcely out of his teens without any idea of what real love was, and Kylie had been only eighteen.

They were grown now, their feelings those of adults. They had each seen much, perhaps too much, of the world, and knew what they wanted and what they didn't. His feelings were those of a man who loved a beautiful, strong woman. How could he not? Kylie was everything he'd ever dreamed of, so much so that he wondered if he could ever be worthy of her.

But Kylie was vulnerable, and he was loath to take advantage of her. She had been right when she'd said it—this thing between them, whatever it was—wasn't smart, not when their enemies were circling them, but he was tired of playing it smart. He wanted to keep on holding her, to absorb the scent of her, to feel her softness.

"You ought to get some sleep," Kylie said. "You're still recovering." Her voice was gentle. She lifted her hand, as if to stroke his cheek, but abruptly dropped it at her side.

He resisted the impulse to take her fingers in his and focused on the practical. "Eat first, then rest." SEAL Rule Number One: eat when you can because you don't know when you'll get another opportunity. "I don't know if I said thank you for saving my life."

"You told me." She smiled. "More than once."

"You could have left. No one would have blamed you." It was important that he get that out.

Her brow furrowed. "Is that what you think of me? That I'd leave you?"

"No. Of course not." He shook his head. "I was just pointing out that you were a hero back there in the mountains."

"I believe the word is *heroine*," she said lightly.

He smiled. "Take the compliment. I'll get started on lunch."

"Why don't I put together some food and you sit down?"

He didn't argue. He knew he had pushed it

today and was now dragging. His body was protesting in exhaustion.

"Thanks. We both need food and rest. Tomorrow, we're going after the people who're trying to kill us."

Kylie moved close, caught his gaze. "We're safe."

"Yes." But he saw the question in her eyes.

For how long?

TWELVE

During the night, Kylie thought of what to do with the SD card. She and Josh needed to find a place to stash it. Going to the police with a story about the lieutenant governor and a mob boss conspiring together would probably get them laughed out of the station house. All they had was a picture.

"We need to get that card somewhere safe," Josh said that morning, echoing her thoughts. "What if I give it to Luca to take to S&J? They'll keep it safe."

"If all of S&J are like Luca and Matt, then count me in." She chewed on her lip.

"What is it?" he asked.

"I want to visit my former editor. She knows more about what's going on in Denver than anyone I can think of. Maybe she'll have some ideas about how McCrane and Winslaw are connected."

"Who is she?"

"I told you about her. Bernice Kyllensgaard.

I was one of her staffers for seven years." Kylie smiled at the thought of her take-no-prisoners editor. She had been on staff at the newspaper until after she was released from the prison camp and had decided to go freelance.

"Kyllensgaard. Scandinavian?"

"That's right. With some German mixed in."

Josh nodded. He called Luca, explained that they needed something safeguarded and asked if he'd pick it up. The former ranger agreed and arrived within the hour.

"I'm gonna owe you big-time when this is all over," Josh said and clapped his friend on the back.

"Don't think I won't remind you of it," Luca said and then took off.

After a quick breakfast, Josh and Kylie drove one of the trucks provided by S&J to the office of Denver's biggest newspaper. The paper had once occupied a huge building that had bustled with activity. The current one was barely two stories high, a sad comedown compared to the block-long, six-story establishment that had once housed the paper.

Kylie understood that print media was a dinosaur compared to online sources of information, but it was still an eye-opener to see what had become of one of the most respected papers in the state.

When they were shown to the editor's office, Kylie introduced Josh to Bernice, then explained why they were there.

Bernice's eyes wore a troubled look by the time Kylie had finished.

"You can see what we're up against," Kylie said.

Her former boss's mouth was a grim line. "What are you two doing to keep yourselves safe?"

"We're going after McCrane and Winslaw," Josh answered. "It's time we turned the tables, and the hunted become the hunters."

"Do you have any ideas of how we can get the goods on them?" Kylie asked. She knew her friend was tapped into the movers and the shakers of the city. Bernice was fond of saying that if she didn't know something, it wasn't worth knowing.

Bernice tapped a finger to her chin. "There's a rumor going around that McCrane has a girlfriend over on the east side of the city. You might start with her."

"He's married," Kylie said and then felt like a fool for stating the obvious.

Bernice shot her a don't-be-naive look. "So he's married. What's your point?"

"Do you have a name and an address for this woman?" Josh asked.

The older woman nodded. "Let me make some calls and get back to you."

Kylie gave her the number of her burner phone.

"You two take care of yourselves," Bernice said and leaned forward to kiss Kylie's cheek.

Kylie gave her a warm embrace. "Thank you. For everything."

"Your friend seems to have a lot of connections," Josh said when they were outside.

"She's been in the business a long time." Kylie's stomach chose that moment to growl. "We'd better feed me before I get hangry."

"Hangry pretty well describes me, too."

They picked up burgers and fries at a fast-food place and then pulled into a deserted park to eat in the car.

"Genuine American burgers and fries were one of the things I missed most when I was deployed," Josh said after polishing off one burger and starting on another. "We could get them in some countries, but we were whistling in the wind in others when it came to finding a good old-fashioned burger and fries."

"I know what you mean. There's enough fat and grease in this bag to clog our arteries for a year."

"Good." And though his eyes were still worried, the darkness in them had lifted. "Happens I like clogged arteries."

She smiled. "So do I."

After the time in the mountains when hunger had constantly gnawed at her stomach, she wanted to down the burger in two bites, but she took her time, savoring every morsel. "This is the best hamburger I've ever had," she said with lip-smacking appreciation.

He grinned. "When you're right, you're right."

Just as they were polishing off the last of the fries, Bernice called.

"The girlfriend's name is Gemma Hardin." When Bernice gave the address, Kylie motioned for Josh to write it down. "Thanks, Bernice. You've been a big help."

"Take care."

The lighthearted conversation of moments ago died as she started the ignition and they got on their way. The knowledge that killers were after them and they had a job to do tended to take the fun right out of the day.

Kylie drove to what had once been a run-down area that had resembled a war zone. Last she'd passed through here, small cookie-cutter houses lined the streets, plastic toys lay in the yards and rusted cars sat on blocks. Drug buys and gang fights had been commonplace. A few old-timers and those who couldn't afford to move away had remained, refusing to leave their decades-old homes.

Now, gentrification was taking place, turning what had been a haven for street people and addicts into an upscale place of boutiques, coffee shops and high-rent apartment buildings that had the advantage of being within walking distance of a number of services.

"The neighborhood has really come up in the world," Kylie said. Though she approved of the improvements, she couldn't help worrying over the older residents who could no longer afford the expensive area but had nowhere else to go. What happened to them?

The trouble with gentrification was that it made life unaffordable for a neighborhood's original residents. The city fathers had promised to find a solution, but that had largely been forgotten as the tax base grew and people rushed in to claim the trendy refurbished lofts, homes and condos.

"It's pretty enough," Josh agreed. "But I can't help wondering where the gangs and drug buys have moved to."

She nodded. Gang activity and the drug business wouldn't stop; they were only shunted off to a new place. She checked the address he'd written down and pointed to one of the new multiuse buildings.

"There."

They found a parking space not too far away

and walked to the pretty building that boasted a bistro, hair salon and other businesses on the ground floor. They took the elevator to the floor where Hardin's apartment was listed.

"You won't find her," a lady who appeared to have just returned from grocery shopping said, juggling her bags while reaching for her keys. "Gemma moved out a couple of weeks ago."

"Would you know where she went?" Kylie asked.

"No. We weren't close. Knew each other enough to say hi, but that was about it." The lady tucked her tongue between her teeth, a considering expression on her face. "But you might check with her veterinarian. She had a cat she loved to distraction. I remember her saying once that she would need to board it while she got settled in a new place."

"Do you happen to know the name of the vet?" Josh asked.

"No. But she said it wasn't far from here." The woman shrugged. "Sorry. That's all I can tell you."

"Thank you," Kylie said. "You've been a big help."

She and Josh returned to their car and searched vet offices in the area. They found one only six blocks away.

Just as she turned the ignition, a gray sedan drove by, windows open.

Josh reacted first. "Get down!"

Gunfire cracked the truck window, two bullets imbedding themselves in the upholstery. Fortunately, neither she nor Josh were hit, but glass shards from the driver's side window rained down on her.

Still shaking, she stayed hunched over.

Josh reached for her hand and closed his fingers around hers. "You okay?"

She didn't answer immediately, still trying to process what had just happened. "I'm fine." But when she touched her face, her fingers came away bloody. "I don't know about you, but I'm tired of being somebody's target."

There was a look of ferocity in his eyes. "We're going to change that."

Josh hovered as an EMT treated the cuts on Kylie's face and neck and wished it had been him who had been sitting in the driver's seat. He had sustained a few cuts, but she had taken the brunt of it.

His lungs constricted to the point of pain that she'd been put in danger yet again.

"You were fortunate that none of those cuts went deeper," the young woman said. "It could have been a lot worse."

The police drilled both him and Kylie about

what had happened. Josh did his best to hold back his impatience.

No, they didn't know who took the shot at them.

Yes, they saw the car, a gray sedan.

No, they didn't get the plates as they were too busy ducking bullets and trying not to get killed.

Yes, they'd make themselves available for further questions if necessary. Not for the first time, he questioned his resistance in telling the police about McCrane and Winslaw's involvement, but it came back to the matter of proof. One photo didn't prove that the lieutenant governor and the mobster were involved in any kind of nefarious scheme, much less that they had orchestrated the attacks on Kylie and himself.

If the police were compromised, he and Kylie couldn't go to them too early without hard evidence of what was happening. And why. They needed something that was too big for dirty cops to sweep under the rug.

He knew that McCrane and Winslaw were guilty, but convincing the police was another matter.

The last thing he wanted was to draw attention to himself and Kylie. Better to stay under the radar until they found the proof they needed.

By the time they were finished, both he and Kylie were more determined than ever to find

McCrane. That started with finding his girlfriend, which started at the vet's office.

They walked into the office and found it packed with anxious pet parents waiting to have their dog or cat and even a bull python seen by the doctor. Fortunately, no one was waiting at the front desk, so Josh headed there and explained to the receptionist that they were trying to find out if Gemma Hardin had boarded her cat there and, if so, could he get her contact information.

"I'm sorry, we can't give out that information," the twentysomething girl said in the voice of someone who was trying to sound professional but was probably a very new hire.

"Thanks anyway," Josh said, and taking Kylie's elbow, they walked outside. "I've got a friend at S&J who can find any information we want."

Thirty minutes later, they had a current location on McCrane's girlfriend.

They found Gemma in a small rented house on the west side of the city. The neighborhood looked like it had seen better days, with houses in need of paint, and trash stirred by the wind, dancing in the street.

After trying the doorbell and getting no response, Josh rapped sharply on the door. The curtains at the front window fluttered before the door was cautiously opened.

Gemma Hardin kept the chain on the door as

she stared out at Josh and Kylie. Both her eyes were circled by faint bruises that looked to be a couple of weeks old.

"Who are you?" she asked in a voice that was probably meant to sound aggressive but came across as scared. "And what do you want?"

"Someone who wants to see George McCrane put away," Josh said. "From the look of you, you may be wanting the same thing."

Self-consciously, she touched her right eye and then her left. "This? This was my fault."

"Did McCrane tell you that?" Kylie asked softly. "Did he tell you that he had to hit you because you did something wrong?"

"No. I fell. That's all." The uneasiness in Gemma's gaze gave the lie to her words.

"Are you sure?" Kylie asked. "You don't look it. And that bruise looks like it was made by a man's fist." Kylie kept her distance to avoid scaring the woman off, but she didn't break Gemma's gaze as she said, "You deserve better. You don't have to be any man's punching bag."

"What business is it of yours?" the other woman demanded.

Kylie didn't have to search for the answer. "It's every woman's business when she sees another woman who's been beaten."

Josh tucked his hands in his pockets. "Can we come in? Get out of the cold."

Gemma looked uncertain. "I guess so." But she made no move to unchain the door.

"Is McCrane the reason you left your apartment and moved out here?" Kylie asked. "There's no shame in being afraid. Especially not of a man like that."

Gemma looked like she wanted to answer, was even about to answer, when a shot rang out. Gemma's face went slack as the bullet bored into the side of her head. Another struck her in the chest.

Josh sprang into action. "Help me pull her inside," he said.

When she didn't move, he started to bark out the order and then saw her face. She was in shock. He should have realized. The sight of someone being gunned down could well trigger a PTSD episode.

He kicked the door aside with enough force to snap the chain lock and pulled Gemma's body into the house, at the same time motioning for Kylie to stay low. He slammed the door shut before feeling for a pulse. He found none.

"She's gone."

More shots sounded, peppering the front door and piercing the air with cracks much like those of fireworks. If he was correct, there were at least two different kinds of weapons being fired. That meant two shooters. Maybe more. He and Kylie were seriously outgunned. This wasn't gunfire from ordinary handguns. The rapid fire reminded him of battles overseas where machine guns were employed.

"We're in big trouble," Kylie said. She seemed to be coming round.

"Tell me something I don't know."

He regretted his sarcasm, but he was worried over how they'd get out of this. They couldn't compete with the rapid-fire shots thrown their way. The only way out was to take the men out and to do it quickly. McCrane seemed to have an unlimited number of men at his disposal.

"Call 911," Josh said. "Tell them that there are multiple shooters. And tell them to hurry."

Josh crouched low by a window, opened it enough that he could return fire. He kept the shooters busy, but they had far greater fire-power than he did. What happened when they advanced? He and Kylie couldn't just sit here.

He and the shooters traded shots, but it was getting them nowhere. He handed Kylie his backup piece. "Can you keep them busy?"

"Where are you going?"

"I want to circle around behind them and take them by surprise."

She looked like she wanted to object but only nodded.

He let himself out by a rear door and, keeping low, did a wide loop around where he'd roughly placed the shooters. If his calculations were correct, he should come upon them from the back.

With Kylie returning fire, they wouldn't know that he had slipped away.

The rev of a motorcycle engine told him that one man had taken off. If possible, he wanted to take the remaining man alive. He found the shooter where he'd guessed and crept up behind him. Something must have alerted the man, for he spun and turned his weapon on Josh. Josh didn't give him time to use it. Instead, he kicked it from the man's hands.

He could have shot the man right there, but he wanted to take him alive and question him. He and Kylie needed answers before they went to the authorities.

The two men fought for control. His opponent was on the small side, but he had a wiry strength to him and managed to hold his own against Josh's larger frame.

"You're a big 'un," the man said. "I'll give you that. Too bad your fighting doesn't live up to your size."

Josh didn't bother replying. He'd learned over the years that there were two kinds of fighters: those who talked a good fight and those who remained silent and then put your lights out.

When Josh lashed out with his good leg, catching the other man behind the knee, the man fell but not without taking Josh with him by grabbing his arm and dragging him down to the ground. Ordinarily, he'd have been able to withstand the other man's tactic, but his injured leg was still not up to full strength.

They wrestled there on the snow-covered ground. For every blow Josh delivered, his opponent matched it with one of his own. Though he wanted to take the man alive, it might not be possible. While he was deployed, he'd killed more of the enemy than he wanted to count. Wartime had its own rules. What of now, though? The question plagued him with relentless persistence.

In the end, he accepted that he might well have to kill again if he were to protect the woman he loved. He didn't have time to ponder over that. Just when he thought he had bested the man, the shooter slipped from Josh's grasp and took off running.

Josh started after him, but his opponent's lead plus his own weakened leg left him hopelessly outpaced. With the man went the only lead they had.

Something on the ground caught his attention, and he bent to pick up a gray-colored mechanism. When he recognized what it was, things shifted into place. Like how their pursuers' semiautomatics had the firepower of a machine gun.

He hurried back to the house and saw that Kylie had placed a blanket over Gemma Hardin.

She grabbed him and hugged him hard. "You're all right. I didn't…" She gulped back a sob and then, obviously aware of what she'd done, pulled back. "I thought you'd been shot. Maybe even killed." Her shuddering breath told its own story of her worry.

"I'm okay." Unnecessarily, he added, "They got away."

"It doesn't matter." Her voice shook ever so slightly. Was it concern for him?

He wanted to ponder the idea, but now wasn't the time. He put it away. For now.

"You're all right. That's all that matters."

Her voice had steadied. He wanted to tell her just what her words meant to him, to let her know that he felt the same about her, but he couldn't find the words. They'd each been through an ordeal in the mountains only to survive and find that it wasn't over. If anything, the targets on their backs had grown larger. She knew that as well as he did and didn't need to hear it. So he kept quiet. There'd be a day when he'd tell her what he felt. But not now.

Instead, he held the polymer device out for Kylie to study.

"What is it?" she asked.

"A Glock switch. It turns an ordinary handgun into a mini machine gun." A spark of satisfaction streaked through him at the discovery of what this was all about, but the satisfaction was short-lived as he realized what trafficking in Glock switches meant.

Kylie's expression flashed from excitement to alarmed comprehension. "That's why it felt like we were in a war zone."

"Exactly. A weapon that's been modified with one of these bad boys can have a rate of fire of 1200 rpm."

She held out a hand, and he gave it to her. "It looks like it's plastic, but it doesn't feel like it."

"It's a polymer compound, probably made on a 3D printer."

"So anyone with a 3D printer could make one." The dawning horror in her voice echoed his own feelings. Turning out Glock switches would be chillingly easy. Gang warfare would turn into battlefields if these got out, not to mention what would happen if warring countries got their hands on them. Even a small militia could rule the battlefield with Glock switches turning ordinary weapons into machine guns.

"They weren't using these when we came out of the vet's office."

"No. This kind of firepower would be bound to attract the police. The shooters followed us here and then opened up on us. A dozen of these could turn a street shooting into a massacre," he said. "Multiply that by a hundred. Or a thousand." It wouldn't take much to produce the switches in terms of time or money. Making them on a 3D printer would be ridiculously easy.

Kylie visibly shuddered. "We'd have a war zone right here in middle America."

"That's right."

"Is this what it's all been about?" she asked. "Covering up a Glock switch operation?"

"There may be more yet. It could be a full-out weapons operation, selling them here and overseas.

"We agreed that Winslaw was mega-rich," Josh continued, "but there's money. And then there's *money*. Winslaw has never made any secret that he's ambitious. There are rumors he's after the governor's seat. From there, he could ride it all the way to Washington. That kind of ambition takes money. Lots and lots of money."

"But to sell weapons? If it ever got out…" She stopped, a stunned look crossing her face.

"Now you're getting it. He can't afford for this to get out. Neither of them can. That's why they want the card. That's why they're willing to kill for it."

"Why did those men take off then?"

"I don't know." He and Kylie couldn't afford to be questioned by the police again. Twice in one day was too much of a coincidence.

He grabbed her hand. "C'mon. We're getting out of here before the police show up."

Spent both emotionally and physically, they headed back to the safe house. They both needed rest. They'd just had a major break in the case, a cause for celebration, but the discovery of the Glock switch painted a grim picture.

THIRTEEN

A morgue didn't care how cold it was outside. It was still colder inside the sterile room with its equally sterile appointments. Josh had been in far too many of them. An occupational hazard.

An overhead fluorescent light cast the room into shadows, giving an eerie impression. Cinder-block walls and shelves of stainless steel trays with stainless steel instruments only added to the air of gloom. The overall effect was one of cold efficiency.

And death.

A day had passed since Gemma Hardin had been gunned down. Josh had wanted to be at the autopsy, and though he'd discouraged Kylie from coming, she'd insisted on accompanying him.

The medical examiner was there, meticulously washing instruments at a sink, then drying them on a precisely folded white towel. She didn't look up until she had finished her task. When she did, her face was unsmiling.

Josh had known Doris Dunnaway for several years. She was in her normal uniform of scrubs, white lab coat and Crocs. The no-nonsense doctor didn't mince words; nor did she pretty them up when reporting facts. Ordinarily, civilians weren't allowed in the morgue, but Doris had made an exception for him. She was friendly with a number of S&J operatives, who often came from various law enforcement backgrounds.

"A hollow point," she said. "Dumdums. We won't be able to match it to any other bullets. It destroyed itself along with any brain matter and anything else it came into contact with."

Josh understood the jargon. Dumdums were a particularly nasty kind of bullet, meant to obliterate their target.

Whoever shot Gemma knew what he was doing.

His attention shifted to Kylie, who was making small mewls of distress while trying valiantly to hide them. He had visited enough morgues that the odor of death no longer bothered him as it once had. Not so Kylie, who looked distinctly green.

He'd attended other autopsies. Too many. It never got easier. If anything, it only got harder, especially when it was that of a young woman who should have had her whole life ahead of her.

The ME pulled a small tin of eucalyptus-scented salve from her pocket and handed it to Kylie. "Put a little of this under your nose. It'll help."

She did as suggested and smiled weakly. "Thanks."

"Anything else you can tell us about Ms. Hardin, Doc?" Josh asked.

"She was nine weeks pregnant." At this, the doctor's voice became pinched, as though the words were hard to get out.

Josh gave a low whistle.

"I can identify the fetus's paternity if I have something to match it to," she continued, voice back to its usual brisk tone. "Give me something—a hair, a coffee cup—anything belonging to the father."

Josh knew her well enough to realize that her cold manner did not mean she didn't care. It allowed her to view the results of the unspeakable acts people committed against each other without losing her professionalism and her ability to do her job. One day, he'd found her weeping after finishing an autopsy upon a six-year-old child killed in a drive-by shooting. He'd never mentioned it to her, knowing she would have been mortified upon learning he'd seen her that way.

He nodded. "Understood."

After a few more minutes, he hustled Kylie out of there. He should never have brought her, but she'd insisted. Aside from that, he didn't want to leave her alone. Their enemies were closing in.

"Pregnant," she said once they were outside. She shivered, and he knew it was not only from the cold. "Gemma must have been terrified. She knew that McCrane couldn't let that get out. No wonder she went into hiding. And we brought her killers right to her door.

"I really want this guy," she finished fiercely. "More than ever now. But first I want a shower to wash off the smell of death."

He understood. He also knew that the stink of death didn't wash away, but he didn't tell her that. They returned to the safe house, where they showered and changed clothes.

An hour later, he said, "Let's make some coffee."

Kylie nodded. "Okay."

He brewed a pot for the two of them, and they settled down at a table with a laptop, one the safe house was equipped with.

He sensed her impatience as he scrolled through several years of newspapers.

"What're you looking for?"

"Here." He pointed to an article from several years back about the closing of a plastics manufacturing factory. Further reading showed that the facility was owned by Winslaw. Things started to click into place.

"Winslaw owned a plastics factory. When plastic got a dirty reputation, the factory went under, but it wouldn't take much to retrofit it to make Glock switches."

Kylie bent over his shoulder to read from an article in the business section of the paper. "'Twenty-thousand-square-foot factory closed with over five hundred workers laid off.' I think we ought to pay a visit."

"I think you're right."

Kylie felt the familiar exhilaration of tracking down a hot lead.

The idea that Winslaw and McCrane were selling Glock switches and weapons on the black market was a terrifying one. Anyone with enough money, including terrorists like those who had kidnapped her, could buy the goods and equip their own private army.

It wouldn't take a lot to manufacture the Glock switches, but they would sell for astronomical amounts of money.

"Winslaw and McCrane could already be selling the switches," Josh said. "That means big money coming in."

Follow the money was a cliché, but it had been proven true over and over. "Where does all the money go?" she wondered aloud. "It has to show up somewhere. They can't just hide that kind of money. Not with all the regulations in place."

Something nagged at the back of her mind, something about another of Winslaw's business ventures. Then she had it. She recalled reading about him recently buying a strip mall. Such a purchase seemed out of his purview until she remembered that it held a laundromat and a dry cleaner's. "They're laundering it. Literally. Laundromats make great places to funnel money." She told Josh about the strip mall, which also contained a nail salon, a gaming arcade and a couple of low-end restaurants.

"All quick turnover businesses," Josh said in a musing tone. "All good places to exchange dirty money for clean. The money's almost impossible to trace. By the time the authorities catch on, the dirty money has disappeared and all that is left are legitimate businesses turning a small but steady profit."

"Why haven't the feds caught on before? An operation this big is bound to have attracted notice."

"I'm sure it has. Could be they don't have sufficient proof. Or they were bought off." His pause told her that he was reluctant to finish what he'd been about to say. "Or killed off."

She let that last sink in but didn't react. "You sound like you know what you're talking about."

"I've been fighting bad guys most of my adult life. The plot doesn't change, only the characters and the scenery." The weariness in his voice told her that he had seen too much of the world's evil.

"We still don't have proof that they're behind all of this," she said. "All we have are some guesses."

"Educated guesses," he reminded her.

"That and five dollars will get you a cup of coffee."

"You're out of touch," he said, grinning. "Coffee is over six dollars now."

The factory was located in a formerly robust industrial area. Now it, along with other businesses, had been abandoned. Plywood replaced what had probably been giant maws in the walls, once occupied by windows. Gang graffiti marred the cinder blocks. It was a depressing sight.

Josh drove around back to park. No sense in advertising their presence.

"What do we expect to find here?" she asked. There was no sign of any activity, legal or illegal. Her excitement took a nosedive. Had they been wrong in thinking that Glock switches were being manufactured here?

"I don't know," Josh admitted.

The place looked like the abandoned factory it was purported to be with one exception: the doors were bolted with brand-new heavy-duty locks. "Why spend the money on new locks for an abandoned building?" she asked. Her senses came alive. Maybe they were on the right track after all.

"Maybe because it's not abandoned," he said.

They circled the building and found that part of the plywood covering a window had been ripped away. Josh pried the rest of it off. He lifted her up and swung her over the window ledge, then followed.

Kylie blinked in the dim light. At first glance, the building appeared empty, but then she saw rows of machinery stacked in a far corner. It didn't appear that production had started. Yet. Pallets held thick sheets of plastic. The same color as the Glock switch.

Had it been a prototype, a first of more to come?

She did a rough calculation of how many Glock switches could be made from the amount of plastic and the resulting mayhem. The loss of life was incalculable.

"Looks like they're getting ready to go operational soon," she said.

Josh put a finger to his lips and pointed to the front of the building. The click of metal against metal told her that someone was opening the front doors.

She looked to the window, but he shook his head. No time.

They hid behind a pile of what looked like discarded machinery.

"The boss isn't gonna like that you used the switch on the lady journalist and that guy," they heard a man say.

"Doesn't matter," another responded. "They'll be dead soon enough."

A coarse laugh ensued. "When you're right, you're right." The first man made a hissing noise. "That window," he said. "It was boarded up earlier, wasn't it?"

"Yeah. Come to think of it, it was."

A pause. "We know you're here," the guy called out. "Might as well show yourselves."

She heard the men's footsteps echo across the space as they began searching. It was only a matter of time before they discovered Kylie and Josh's hiding place.

"Well, lookie who I found here," the first man said, stumbling upon them. His partner joined him.

Josh and Kylie stood. "Get out of here," he said. When Josh motioned for her to move behind him, she refused and stepped out so that she faced the two men.

"I told you to get out of here," Josh repeated.

"I don't take orders from you," Kylie retorted. "They're two of them. You need me."

She took the measure of the man who had appeared to single her out. The other man faced off with Josh.

"One thing you can say about McCrane and Winslaw is that they have friends in low places," she said to nobody in particular.

The men cackled out rough-sounding laughs.

"We could shoot you right now," the smaller man said.

"You could," she agreed, "but then you'll never get what's on my camera. That's what you want, isn't it? I don't imagine your boss will be very happy with you."

He appeared to think about it. "I could break every bone in your body."

"Could you? You look to me like someone who's all hat and no cattle."

A scowl replaced his smirk. The time for wordplay was over. Her man came in hard and fast. She sidestepped, gratified when his own momentum carried him to the ground.

"You like playing, little girl?" the man asked upon picking himself up.

"I like winning."

He swept out his leg and tried to trip her, but she danced out of the way. So far he'd only been testing her. Now would come the real fight.

Josh would have his hands full with his man; she couldn't depend upon him to come to her aid. This was her fight.

When the thug reached for her this time, he found his target. So large were his hands that the expanse between his thumb and little finger completely circled her neck. He could crush her windpipe if she didn't escape his grasp within the next few seconds.

She brought her knee up and aimed for his groin. *Nailed it.*

Immediately, he released her. The agony she read in his gaze told her she'd gotten in a good blow, but would it be enough to get him to back off?

She had her answer in a second when he advanced once more, grabbed her hair and slammed her head into the wall. The man probably outweighed her by eighty or more pounds. He'd obviously been combat trained. When he threw a punch at her neck, she dodged and took it on her shoulder instead. Pain sang down her arm all the way to her fingers.

She couldn't let it stop her. Her life depended on it, as well as Josh's—she had to keep this man from joining the attack on him.

If she could only hold out until Josh finished off his opponent. She dared not look his way, not wanting to distract him. Plus, she needed to fix all of her attention on the man who looked like he was only getting started on her.

She twisted her leg around his ankle and yanked forward. When he fell, she fell with him, but she was prepared and rolled away as soon as they hit the ground. She didn't stay down.

He wanted to play rough? Well, so could she. She was on him, delivering blows, one after another. Some he managed to dodge, others he took. She smelled blood. His and hers.

For a half a moment, her vision grayed from where he'd slammed her head against the wall. Pain throbbed through the side of her head, and she kept consciousness through sheer will.

Shake it off.

Fury screamed through her, and she jammed her fingers into his eyes. He yowled. She followed up with a fist to the underside of his chin.

He staggered back. When his phone suddenly chirped with the notification of a text, he pulled it out and glanced at it. "We gotta go," he told his partner. The man speared her with a hate-filled glare. "Another time, sweetheart."

"You okay?" Josh asked her after the men hurried out.

The side of her head still rang from the nasty blow she'd taken.

"Kylie." The alarm in his voice had her squaring her shoulders.

"I'm fine."

"Must have been something important to have them tearing out of here," he said.

"Like McCrane calling them to another job. I can't say I'm disappointed. My guy was about to mop the floor with me."

"Don't sell yourself short. You were a real tiger." He paused. "You could have taken off, but you held your own and then some."

At his words, a surge of pride swept through her, and she pumped her fist in the air.

Her flash of victory dissipated, and she expelled a breath slowly. "Is this ever going to be over?"

"It will be. We just have to hang on."

She wished she believed that.

Kylie's words stayed with him as he drove. She had been right when she'd voiced aloud her fear that the goon who'd attacked her would have been mopping the floor with her in another minute.

He couldn't keep putting her in jeopardy, but how was he to keep her safe?

"Let me take you away," he said. "Put you somewhere safe. I'll come back and deal with McCrane and Winslaw." Even as he said the words, he knew she wouldn't agree.

But he had to try.

"You know that's not going to work," she said,

shaking her head. "They won't give up until they have what they want. It's not just the SD card. They want me, and they want me dead."

"Don't you trust me? I said I'd take care of them."

"I trust you more than anyone I know." Her sigh tore at his heart. She sounded infinitely weary. At the same time, there was hard resolve in her eyes.

One of the things he most admired about her was her indomitable spirit. She wasn't going to give this up. No matter what.

"You've done more for me than I had a right to ask. And I wouldn't blame you if you wanted out. But I'm sticking around," she said. "I won't run. I can't. If I do, I'll never be able to trust myself again." She heaved out a breath, as though the words had cost her the last of her remaining energy.

"You aren't responsible for bringing down a crime syndicate or a corrupt politician. Write the story, take the pictures, but let the professionals handle it." The words were right, but he heard the pleading in them. The last thing he felt like right now was a professional. His feelings for Kylie had mixed him up until he didn't recognize himself.

"Someone has to stand up and say 'enough.'"

"It doesn't have to be you."

"Why not?" she challenged.

She had him there. "Because…"

"Because why?"

He couldn't tell her. Didn't have the words. The truth was that he was falling for her all over again. Or maybe he'd never stopped loving her. And didn't think he'd survive if she was hurt. Or worse.

Kylie clasped her hands in her lap. "I'm not going anywhere."

He'd known that, but he'd had to try. His only option now was to protect her at all costs.

FOURTEEN

Back at the S&J safe house, Kylie fixed supper. It was simple fare, a can of chili and a cornbread mix she'd taken from the pantry. She and Josh ate heartily and then cleaned up together.

"You're being awfully quiet," she said.

"Lots to think about."

"Want to share?"

"Maybe later. I'm still trying to get it straight in my mind. When I do, I'll let you know."

He bent to put dirty dishes in the dishwasher. When he straightened, he stood as rigid as the soldier he'd been. It did her heart good to see it. Despite not knowing what they would do next, despite still having targets on their backs, despite everything, she smiled.

Knowing Josh hadn't suffered any permanent effects from the infection was all that mattered. The rest of the stuff, they'd take one day at a time. Even though her body was ready to collapse, her brain wouldn't shut down. Questions buzzed through her mind.

Apparently, his mind was equally occupied. "Who knew we were going to see Gemma Hardin?"

Kylie had asked herself the same question.

"Bernice," she answered reluctantly. "But it's not a big stretch to think that we might be looking for Gemma. Anyone who knew McCrane was keeping a girlfriend on the side could have guessed that would be our next move. We could have been followed from the paper."

"But not just anyone gave us the address where we were shot at."

She could see what he was angling at but… "Bernice wouldn't set us up. Why would she?" Kylie refused to believe that her friend would set her up to be killed. Bernice had given Kylie her first real break in the business. It had been Bernice who had encouraged her to take her work overseas and tell the stories that no one else was telling. It had been Bernice who had helped pitch Kylie to other editors when she'd decided to go freelance.

Josh held up a hand, presumably to ward off any more defense of Bernice. "I don't know. What I do know, though, is that she's the one who told us that McCrane had a girlfriend, and she's the one who gave us that address."

Kylie knew Josh was only trying to talk through the possibilities, but that didn't mean she had to like it.

"Bernice gave us Gemma's old address, not the new one," she said.

"That's right," Josh said, "and we were shot at while we were at that address, if you remember."

"And at the new address," Kylie felt bound to point out. "Bernice didn't know anything about that. She couldn't have set us up there."

"You're right. But we could have been followed from Gemma's old place to her new one."

"Bernice believed in me when no one else did," she said. "She gave me my first job. I don't believe she tried to have us killed. I *won't*. We can settle this. We'll go see her tomorrow."

He was shaking his head before she'd even finished speaking. "If I'm wrong, we'll only offend her. And if I'm right, we'll give away the fact that we're onto her."

Kylie nodded, but she didn't like it. She didn't like it at all.

Though they made small talk for a short while, the argument had put a rift between them, sending a chill through the air.

Giving them both space, she headed to one of the bedrooms. She got ready for bed and wished she knew what to do. Not for the first time, the impulse to pray returned. How tempting it was to fold her hands and pour out her heart to the Lord, asking Him to help her and Josh find the answers they needed. If she did so, however, how did she reconcile what she'd experienced in Afghanistan?

Or could she?

Her earlier belief in God had been naive, even simplistic. That belief had sustained her through most of her adult life, but she understood now it wasn't enough. Her faith had needed to grow, to stretch.

She couldn't pretend that the Lord hadn't known what was happening. Nor could she tuck the whole thing away and pretend that she hadn't witnessed such inhumanity. If she did, she would be denying the sacrifice the NGO workers had made and the courage of the villagers. And Ryan's memory.

None of this was helping, and she pushed the questions along with the images they evoked to the back of her mind. Right now, she and Josh had a mystery to solve.

Still, the question persisted in her mind of who else knew they would be at Gemma Hardin's old address at that time. Could this all be a coincidence? It was possible, but she felt it wasn't likely.

Bernice might have talked to someone and inadvertently let it slip. An innocent mistake. Or someone at S&J, someone who knew Josh and

Kylie were using the safe house, could have sold them out.

That didn't feel right either. And she found herself thinking thoughts she didn't like.

Come morning, neither mentioned the disagreement of last night. They tiptoed around each other, verbally and physically. Tension filled the air, making Josh know they had to do something different.

They needed a lead. It was doubtful that Winslaw and McCrane would return to the factory. So where did he and Kylie go from here?

"What do you usually do when you come across a puzzle you can't solve?" Josh asked.

"Start taking it apart. Piece by piece."

"That's what we do here. We start taking it apart. Piece by piece. And then we'll put it back together so that the pieces are in the right place."

"Thanks for being on my side." The words were so soft that he had to strain to hear them.

"There's nowhere else I'd rather be."

The words were out before he could think better of them. Still, he didn't want to take them back. Sharing the last few days with Kylie had made him think of eleven years ago. They had both changed, but his feelings for her hadn't. If anything, they'd grown stronger.

She was no longer a young girl and he a boy

only a few years older. They'd stretched themselves and been tried in ways neither had foreseen.

"You look like you're a thousand miles away," she said.

He shook his head. More like eleven years away. She was even prettier now than she was then, but it wasn't only her beauty that pulled him. It was her integrity, her determination to do the right thing even if it put her in jeopardy, that drew him to her.

It was his job to make certain that it didn't cost her life.

"Can you do a search of all of Winslaw's appearances and activities in the last…let's say… six months?" Josh asked. "I want to get an idea of where he's been, who he's been seeing, anything you can find."

"No problem." Kylie booted up the laptop and started. A first pass didn't reveal anything interesting. The lieutenant governor had visited two veterans who had just celebrated their ninety-ninth birthdays. Nothing there. Then there was a visit to the children's hospital and another to a ribbon-cutting ceremony for a new civic center.

She did another pass, deeper this time. Still nothing. What was she missing? She tried different combinations of words and still couldn't make any connections to McCrane.

She looked up. "Nothing so far, but it isn't going to be anything that shows up right off. Something small, maybe. Something you might not think much of unless you were looking closely."

"If it's that small, how are we going to see it?" he asked.

"Oh, it will stand out once we see it, and we'll wonder why we didn't click on it right away. Once we see it, we won't be able to unsee it."

More research. And still no results. What was she missing? The question taunted her.

Then she saw it. There was a second trip made to the nursing home in which Winslaw had visited several elderly men. That was a goodwill publicity move. There couldn't be anything there… But further reading showed that the LG had made several more trips to the facility. Two faces recurred regularly in photos.

Two men, both ninety-nine according to the article, smiled at the lieutenant governor in one photo. He had wedged himself in between them, with a big birthday cake taking center stage. Other elderly residents in suit jackets crowded the stage around him.

She studied the deeply lined faces of the two men. Given their permission, they'd make wonderful studies for portraits, and she made a mental note to visit the care facility when this was all over.

While one man's eyes wore a vague expression, the other had a piercing gaze that looked like he had seen much of the world and hadn't forgotten a thing.

Her gaze remained riveted on the picture until she grew impatient with herself. But could a ninety-nine-year-old man be involved with what was going on?

"You see something," Josh said. "What is it?"

She pointed to the story on the screen. "I'm not sure. But I keep coming back to it."

She read the story to him. "Winslaw might not be the brightest bulb in the chandelier, but he doesn't waste his time on things that don't matter. So why is he making return visits to this particular place?" And why were there two recurring faces? The photos showed Winslaw with several different men, always clustered together in groups, over the course of his visits. But she'd spotted the same two men in several of the pictures. If it hadn't been for the one man's piercing gaze that had captured her attention, she might not have noticed.

She did a little more digging and came up with the names of the men. Lyle Thompson and Omar Redken.

A deeper search revealed that Redken had been involved in organized crime in the fifties.

"Wow," Josh said, reading over her shoulder. "Looks like he did it all."

The article described how Redken had run Colorado's crime family with an iron fist, only being taken down on tax evasion charges.

"Like Al Capone," she murmured.

"Just like. Redken served twelve years in prison," he read further.

Something scratched at the corner of her memory, something she should remember, but it slipped away. The scratching sensation told her that it was important. But what? She had a feeling that if she could pinpoint it, they might be able to put together more pieces of the puzzle.

"It's time for another road trip," Josh said.

Familiar excitement zinged through her at the thought of tracking down a lead. "When we get to the nursing home, let me take point," she said.

"You can't go."

"What do you mean I can't go?"

"It's too risky." She was about to protest when he continued, "If I'm caught, I can talk my way out of it, or call for backup. If they get you, there's nothing they won't do to get those photos, and after that they'd have no use for you. We need to keep you safe—if we keep you safe, we keep the story safe until you can get it out to the right people."

Emotion clogged her throat. She knew he was

trying to protect her, but maybe he had a point. "Do one thing for me," she asked.

"What's that?"

"Be careful. And come back." *To me*, she nearly added but stopped herself in time.

When had she stopped thinking of Josh as her protector and started thinking of him as the man she wanted to return to her?

FIFTEEN

Josh understood Kylie didn't like being left behind. If the positions had been reversed, he'd have felt the same way, but he couldn't risk her being identified.

The care facility was upscale, posh even, the appointments quietly elegant, the staff courteous and helpful.

When he was shown to a table in the dining room where he was told Mr. Redken sat, he noted the domed plate covers, fine silverware and fresh flowers. It appeared the residents lived the good life.

"Mr. Redken, I'm Jake Greene, a graduate student doing my dissertation on organized crime," he said. "I was hoping you would give me your impressions."

Redken looked up and stuck out his hand. "Omar Redken." His gaze moved over Josh, seeming to miss little. "Little long in the tooth to be a student, aren't you?"

When undercover, Josh had always found it best to stick to the truth as much as possible. He had anticipated that and gave a rueful shrug. "I did a stint in the military. When I came back, I wanted to go in a different direction. Got my master's in political science and am now working on my dissertation in organized crime."

The elderly man subjected him to another long study, then gestured for an attendant to pull up a chair. "Sit if you have a mind to listen to an old man relive his past."

Redken asked Josh a series of questions, then nodded when he answered as though satisfied. "Colorado in the fifties was wide open for organized crime. Those were the days."

Josh sat back and listened as Redken talked at length about his life as one of the major players in Denver's wild and woolly days.

"We did it all," Redken said. There was no boasting in the words, only a statement of fact.

"I was one of the best," he concluded after telling story after story of bank robberies, embezzlement, money laundering, you name it. "Never was caught for any of that. It was tax evasion that took me down. Did my time. Now I'm enjoying my 'retirement.'" He winked at the last.

Josh wanted to bring up Winslaw, but he didn't want to push the old man and steered the conversation to family. "Does your family come see you often?"

Redken smiled proudly. "I have a grandson who is making his own mark in the state. He's in state government."

Winslaw…that was the connection. Josh tried to appear casual. "Oh?"

The man nodded. "His father, my son, was born on the wrong side of the blanket, as we used to say. He took his mother's name. They both stayed out of the rackets, I'm proud to say.

"He likes to hear stories about the old days. He asks a lot of questions, always listens to the answers like he's really interested. I was something back then. Me and my boys ran the city, most of the state. We played rough, sure, but we had a code. We never hurt women or children, not like the scum who run things today. There's no honor in what they do. No honor at all."

Josh wondered if he knew his grandson was running with people like McCrane—making weapons that would indeed hurt women and children.

"You're fortunate to have a grandson who visits."

"That I am. Some of the folks here have no one who comes to see them. They pretend they don't mind, but you can tell that they do. My grandson didn't always come to visit, but lately he's been real attentive."

A shadow moved into Redken's eyes.

"Is something wrong?" Josh asked.

"He and I didn't part on the best of terms the last time he was here."

"What happened?"

"I told him I was changing my will. I'm leaving my money to this place, a scholarship if you will, to help people who can't afford a decent place to live once they can't live on their own."

In spite of the older man's background, Josh was impressed with Redken's generosity. "That's very decent of you."

"I'm not going to be around much longer. No sense in pretending that I am. I want my money to do some good after I'm gone."

"And your grandson didn't like the idea?" Josh could only imagine Winslaw's reaction.

Redken gave a wry smile. "You could say that. He said that I was stealing from him. As if spending my own money is stealing." The smile was replaced by a look of disgust. "It's not like he and his wife aren't rolling in money as it is. My lawyer's coming tomorrow with the new will. As soon as I sign it, my grandson won't be able to pester me about it anymore."

Josh and Redken continued the conversation until the older man had finished his meal and announced that he was tired. An attendant pushed his wheelchair to his room.

Josh left, eager to share with Kylie what he'd learned, but when he returned to the safe house, it was to find it empty with a note on the table. *Had an errand to run. Be back soon.*

She was all right. He repeated the words until they were burned into his brain, but he still couldn't shake the uneasiness that fell over him like a dark cloud.

Kylie couldn't sit idle. Not when Josh was out tracking down the most promising lead they'd had so far. She had to do something. She'd decided to visit Bernice and lay to rest any doubts about her friend.

Grateful that Luca had left two vehicles for her and Josh, she'd started the remaining truck and set out for the newspaper office. Now she sat in the parked vehicle outside of it. She got out of the truck and entered the building.

"Kylie, I didn't expect to see you today," Bernice said upon greeting her, "but I'm glad you stopped by."

"A lot has happened since I last saw you." Kylie recounted finding Gemma only to have her shot in front of her eyes and then related the incident at the factory.

Upon hearing of the latest events, Bernice

shook her head. "You and your friend sure attract trouble. I'm just glad you're all right."

Kylie smiled. "Me, too." They talked about where her career was headed and future jobs. Everything was normal, and she was glad to put aside her doubts about a woman who had been nothing but good to her.

Her gaze drifted to a degree hanging on the wall behind the desk. Bernice Redken Kyllensgaard.

"Redken," she said aloud. "I remember you telling me that your maiden name was Redken." She had forgotten that until she'd seen the neatly printed name on the document.

Looking puzzled, Bernice nodded. "That's right."

"Any relation to Omar Redken?"

Bernice's body language shifted, and with it, the room filled with a subtle tension that hadn't been there only moments ago. "What do you know about Omar?"

"So you *are* related to him."

"He's my grandfather. Though I can never seem to find the time to see him these days," Bernice said lightly. She smiled but it seemed forced.

"I just heard his name recently." A coincidence. That's all it was, but she recalled years ago her mentor herself saying that there was no such thing as coincidence.

"Where did you hear it?"

Kylie realized she'd gone too far. "I just ran across it somewhere." She made a show of checking her phone for the time. "I'd better get going."

"Stay," Bernice said. Her tone had hardened. "I want to know where you came across the Redken name."

Her friend's words were like a weight in her chest. Kylie tried for nonchalance and stood. "I really don't remember."

"Not so fast." Bernice pulled a gun from her top drawer. "You're too nosy for your own good. That's always been your problem. Too eager to find answers without thinking through where those answers might lead you."

Kylie stared at the woman she'd called friend for seven years. Panic coursed through her. "I don't know what you're talking about."

Bernice eyed her shrewdly. "Oh, I think you do."

Kylie's mind raced, and she knew it was too late to backtrack. So she gave up pretending she didn't understand the significance of the connection. "How could you be involved with Winslaw and McCrane? They're both lowlifes who don't care how many people they kill with their jacked-up weapons."

Bernice laughed coldly. "Money. What else? You think a photojournalist's pay is bad. Trying being an editor. Especially when print media is folding up faster than you can unfold a newspaper.

"There was a time when print journalism was a respected field. Now it's a joke. Online stories appear before we can get a paper out." She flung her arm to indicate the building. "Did you notice that there's scarcely anyone working here? And those who do are all down on the production floor.

"Besides, I decided I was tired of working my butt off for next to nothing. Granville Winslaw is my cousin. When he asked me to throw in my lot with him and McCrane, I went for it. Granville's running for governor next term and needs media backing, even if it is only a washed-up newspaper. He knows I have connections."

"You and Winslaw are cousins," Kylie said, wrapping her mind around all that Bernice had just told her.

"You could say that I'm part of the family business. It doesn't hurt that the business has made us all very, very rich with more to come." She smiled menacingly.

"What happened to you?" Kylie asked in equal parts horror and incredulity.

"I got a large dose of reality. That's what happened. I always knew my family was founded on crime—there was a time when I tried to carve my own path, one of integrity. But look where that got me." She gestured with her free hand. "I'm coming up on retirement and don't intend to eat cat food because I can't afford anything else."

"You call murder getting a dose of reality?" Kylie shook her head, pleading with her eyes. "If you go to the authorities now, I'll go with you. Put in a good word for you. If you turn state's evidence, you may get off with a lighter sentence."

"You always were a Goody Two-shoes. As for your offer, thanks but no thanks. I have no intention of spending time behind bars."

"What are you going to do?"

"I'm going to hand you over to my partners." She motioned with the weapon. "Sit down and stay down. Or I'll take care of you myself."

"You mean kill me."

Bernice shrugged. "If that's what it comes to."

Kylie did as her one-time friend ordered. She needed to play it smart and stay alive.

She looked at the woman she no longer recognized, a woman she'd admired and respected for years, and wondered how she could have been so wrong. "You'd do this? Turn me over to the men who want to kill me? We were friends. Doesn't that mean anything?"

"Not as much as the money I'm going to make once we put the switches into production. I'll be richer than I ever dreamed." She paused, and a whisper of remorse crossed Bernice's face. "Look, Kylie, you're a good photojournalist, and I'm sorry you got caught up in this, but there's nothing I can do."

"You can let me go."

Bernice barked out an unladylike laugh. "Have you heard what McCrane does to people who cross him?"

Kylie knew the man was ruthless.

"If I want to save my own hide, I don't have a choice. After that, it's out of my hands."

Kylie tried to stay calm. "And you think that excuses you?"

Bernice shifted the gun from one hand to the other. "Who's to say? Besides, I've grown accustomed to the good life. How do you think I live the way I do? Do you think my salary covers the BMW and my clothes, the trips abroad?" She made a scoffing motion. "Think again. I couldn't afford a two-story walk-up on what the paper pays me."

Kylie had occasionally wondered how her editor managed to live as she did, but she'd chalked it up to family money—it turned out she'd been partially right.

"Has it all been an act?" Kylie asked. "You helping me with my career? Giving me breaks to get ahead?"

"No." Now Bernice's voice softened. "You reminded me of someone. Someone from a long time ago. She was a little naive but determined to do the right thing, just like you."

"Yourself?"

"Yes. Why the surprised look? I used to have ethics. I was a crusader when I started out in this business. Determined to show the world for what it was and then change it." She looked weary for a moment. "But then I got my eyes opened. The hard way. One of my stories was about the deputy district attorney. He was dirty as they come, and I was going to expose him." She stopped again.

"What happened?" Kylie asked.

"My editor pulled me aside and said that if I kept after that story, I'd alienate not only city hall but every other player in town. I had a choice to make. My career or my self-respect. I chose my career."

So, Bernice had started on this crooked path a long time ago. No wonder she'd agreed to Winslaw's offer. "You always told me to go after the story, no matter whose feathers I might ruffle."

"Maybe I wanted to relive my glory days through you." Bernice waved the gun at Kylie. "Now sit down and shut up before I forget that I liked you once."

Realizing that Josh would have no way to know she'd been here, Kylie tore off the gold chain she was never without and threw it to the ground, kicking it under the desk. Maybe he'd find it. Bernice pulled a roll of packing tape from her desk drawer.

Quickly and efficiently, the older woman bound Kylie's arms and legs to the chair. "Mc-Crane will be here any minute, and then I won't have to look at your eyes so filled with righteous indignation."

"You don't mind that they're going to kill me?"

Bernice lifted a shoulder in a negligent shrug. "Why should I mind? Like I said, I gave up my ethics a long time ago."

Though Bernice had admitted to her guilt, Kylie was still struggling to take it in. How had she been so unaware of the woman's perfidy? Easy. She'd seen what she'd wanted to see.

She'd never thought of herself as naive. Somehow, though, she'd missed the clues about her longtime friend.

She had to try to make the woman see reason. "You would murder me to make a few dollars?"

"A few dollars?" Bernice's laugh grated against Kylie's nerves. "Try a few million dollars. Maybe even more. We're sitting on a gold mine."

"You always valued the truth above all else." Kylie hitched her chin to a plaque above Bernice's desk and read, "'Facts do not cease to exist because they are ignored.'" The Aldous Huxley quote hung there, a silent indictment of what the editor had become.

For a moment, a whiff of regret moved into Bernice's eyes. "That was only so much nonsense. Money and power write their own truth." She sighed. "I'm sorry it came to this. If only you'd kept your nose out of it, everything would have been fine."

Kylie understood there would be no going back from this. Bernice had drawn her line in the sand. "I'm sorry. Sorry for you."

At that moment, McCrane showed up and, with the ease of familiarity, went to a large globe, pressed a button to reveal a small but well-stocked bar, and poured himself a drink.

Kylie had been in the office numerous times over the years but had never known the globe was anything but what it looked like.

"You're a hard person to kill, Ms. Robertson," McCrane said.

"Thank you."

He raised a brow. "It wasn't meant as a compliment."

"Nevertheless, I took it as one."

The sparring was over.

She wanted to fight, to show him, to show all of them, that she wouldn't be taken so easily, but she was bound to the chair, gift wrapped like a present with a bow on top. "I'm not alone."

"I'm counting on that. The ex-SEAL will come charging to your rescue. We'll take him out, as well."

Being used to lure Josh here sent a fiery bolt of acid spilling through her stomach. She should have held her tongue.

Winslaw showed up fifteen minutes later, one of his henchmen at his side. She recognized him as one of the men from the warehouse.

Though it was warm in the room, Winslaw didn't remove his gloves.

"What are you doing here?" Bernice asked.

"Just paying my cousin a visit while I take care of some business." When the lieutenant governor pulled a weapon, Kylie braced herself, but he didn't turn it on her. Instead, he used it on Bernice.

There was a pop, and Kylie couldn't help crying out at seeing Bernice gunned down that way. She wondered that somebody didn't hear the shot and come running, then realized that the shot was muffled. In her fear, she'd missed the suppressor upon first seeing the weapon.

"Good," McCrane said. "We were going to have to get rid of her anyway. She was getting greedy, always wanting more money."

"I can't say that I blame my cousin," the LG said. "It seems that it runs in the family."

McCrane looked annoyed. "What are you talking about?"

Winslaw bent to remove the gun from Bernice's hand. "You know that I studied accounting in school," he said. "One thing I learned is that a pile of money split three ways is a lot less than if that same money stays in one neat pile." Calmly, he put his weapon in McCrane's hand, fired it again, and then picked up Bernice's .38, making the whole thing look like a shoot-out. He didn't rush but took his time as though he was merely moving a pile of papers from one spot to another rather than planning on killing a second person in a matter of minutes.

The mobster didn't look worried, only annoyed. "What are you doing now? Stay focused. We need to move her body."

"Oh, I don't think that'll be necessary," Winslaw said.

"We can't just leave her here."

"Can't we? It'll be perfect. It will appear that you and she killed each other."

Understanding finally dawned in McCrane's eyes, and his expression grew alarmed. "You can't kill me. We're partners."

"Yeah? You were always the one giving orders, thinking you were so much smarter than me. Did you think I didn't overhear you and Bernie making jokes about me, about how ignorant

I was? Well, who's the ignorant one now? And don't bother calling for your men. They're working for me now. Turns out they can be bought if the price is right."

McCrane's eyes widened. "Wait. You're wrong. I never called you—"

The mobster tried to run, but it was too late. Winslaw shot him in the back.

He then placed a decorative pillow against the gun's muzzle, held the gun in Bernice's hand and pressed the trigger, shooting the mobster once more. Seeing Kylie's horror, he only smiled. "The police will assume they shot each other."

"What about me? Are you going to shoot me, too?"

"No. You're not getting off that easy."

Kylie couldn't keep back the tears that gathered in her eyes. Whatever else Bernice had been, she hadn't deserved that.

"Isn't that sweet?" Winslaw mocked. "Too bad it's not going to help. I have to give you credit for staying one step ahead of us, but that's over. If you weren't afraid before, you should be now." The menace in his eyes underscored his words.

Kylie kept her expression impassive. Showing fear wouldn't help. Not with the man who stood over her, a pistol in his hand, gazing at her with contempt.

He ripped off her bindings and, at the last minute, grabbed the pillow he'd used to silence the shot. The man didn't miss a beat. He then hustled her out of the back door of the building but not before assigning the man with him to guard the office.

"A man will probably show up looking for her," he said, pointing at Kylie. "You know what to do with him."

Before shoving her in a car, he tied her hands behind her back with the length of tape he'd taken with him. "You couldn't leave it alone, could you?" he mused aloud. "Just had to find out what was going on. Now you know. Too bad you won't be able to write a story about it. Who knows? It might have earned you a Pulitzer."

She ignored that. Josh would come for her. But would it be in time? She couldn't depend upon being rescued. She had to save herself.

No. That wasn't right. The Lord was with her. He had always been with her, but she'd been too blind, too stubborn, too prideful to see it.

Could He forgive her?

Her heart knew He would. She only wished she hadn't waited so long to understand that He'd never left her.

SIXTEEN

Irritation with Kylie took a hard turn to worry when she wasn't back within an hour. Josh slammed his fist into his palm. The note she'd left told him nothing.

Where had she gone? She hadn't said anything about going somewhere this morning when he'd left. He knew they hadn't left things in a good place between them, but he'd planned on talking through things when he got back.

Didn't she realize she was still in danger?

Then he had it. Yesterday, she'd said that she wanted to go see her mentor. She planned to prove to him and to herself that Bernice wasn't dirty.

Could she really have been so foolish as to confront her friend and ask outright if she was involved in the whole nasty business of weapons trafficking?

Why didn't she wait?

He had only to look at himself to find the answer. He'd practically dared her to prove that her friend wasn't involved. To Kylie, that was as good as a challenge, and she'd never been one to back down from a challenge.

Okay. Take it easy. Could be that she'd gone there just to talk, but he knew better.

What if she'd confronted her editor and the woman had turned on Kylie? It stood to reason that she'd have a backup plan in case anyone ever caught on to her.

When he reached the newspaper office, he was confronted by a burly man who had *hired gun* written all over him. Beneath the bruises and swollen eye, Josh recognized the man as one who had tried to take him and Kylie out in the warehouse.

"Boss said how you'd probably be showing up and that I was to take care of you," the man said. "I've been wanting a rematch with you. We'll see who's the better man."

Josh didn't have time to fool with the thug. "Let's see you do it."

"I could just shoot you, but I want to have some fun with you first." He ran an appraising look over Josh.

The man came at him, fists flying. Though his technique lacked style, he had plenty of muscle behind his punches.

Josh was ready, refusing to allow the injury

to his leg to slow him down. He had two rules when it came to fights. Finish them. And finish them fast. He planted his foot, shot out a fist and served a solid blow to his opponent's nose, smashing it. While the man swiped at the blood pouring down his face, Josh rotated on his other foot and delivered a roundhouse kick to his solar plexus that sent him sprawling.

His opponent grabbed Josh's ankle, pulling him to the floor. Pain screamed through his bad leg, but he ignored it. The two men grappled for dominance until Josh pressed his thumbs against a sensitive spot on the man's neck, rendering him unconscious. He bound his wrists with plastic cuffs and pushed him out of the way.

Inside the office, he found two bodies. The relief that poured through him that neither belonged to Kylie was tempered by questions over whether she'd been there in the first place and where she was now and who had taken her.

A glint of gold caught his eye. He stooped to pick up a thin chain. Kylie's. That answered the question of if she'd been there. He pocketed the chain and prayed he'd be able to give it to her.

He examined the bodies and saw that it was a clumsy setup to make it appear that Bernice and McCrane had killed each other. The police and ME's office would find the truth. He called the police and gave a terse explanation, but despite the order to wait where he was, he took off. He didn't have time to wait around for the authorities to sort things out. He needed to find Kylie.

It didn't take a lot of brain power to know that Winslaw was behind it.

Where would he take Kylie? And then he had the answer. The plastics factory.

"Where are you taking me?" Kylie asked.

"Wouldn't you like to know?"

As Winslaw drove out of town, she recognized the scenery. They were on the way to the plastics factory.

"McCrane and Bernie always thought they were smarter than me," he said. She'd never heard anyone refer to Bernice as Bernie. "I guess I showed them."

The man's arrogance was more than galling, but maybe she could use that against him. Ego was a powerful motivator, especially for someone like Winslaw who used power and cruelty to bring his enemies down.

"How did you and McCrane get involved?"

"McCrane knew I wanted to run for governor and that I needed money. He knew I owned a strip mall as well as the factory and said we could help each other. I didn't want to climb in bed with a mobster, but he kept pushing. Finally, he did some digging and discovered that Omar

Redken is my grandfather. My father never took his old man's name. Never had anything to do with him. I thought the connection was dead and buried. Until McCrane."

"People wouldn't hold it against you. You weren't even born when your grandfather was sent to jail."

"Don't you get it? Dirt sticks. If word got out that I had a mobster in my family tree, I'd be dead politically. McCrane has a way of making people fall into line. Then, when he told me about the Glock switch operation, I changed my tune. Even with a small operation, we've been raking in money hand over fist. Thanks to you, I have to find a new location, but I'll find a new place to set up shop."

"You beat McCrane at his own game."

"I let him think what everyone else does—that I'm not good for anything but playing the fool. Why do you think I was content to do just that? People are careless around fools. They think they don't pay attention to what is being said. I've picked up more juicy tidbits about colleagues and their wives by just staying quiet with a vacuous expression on my face than I ever would by spying on them.

"As for McCrane, all I had to do was bide my time. He thought he was using me, but I was using him. Just like I used the governor."

He smiled indulgently at Kylie. "People think I'm a yes-man, a gofer, but I'm ten times—twenty times—the man the governor is. He does what he's good at—making speeches and kissing babies. The rest, he leaves to me. The arrangement suits us both."

She was impressed by his willingness to play the buffoon. The man had fooled everyone. The governor, his staff, the public. Even McCrane.

"It's too bad you stumbled on our little secret. You're a smart lady, but you were too smart for your own good. That never works out well."

"You're plenty smart, all right," Kylie said. "It's just too bad that you chose to work for the wrong side."

Winslaw stretched his mouth in an ugly smirk. "The wrong side, as you put it, is the power side."

"I don't see it that way."

"No? Like I said, too bad. You could have gone places. Bernie told me about you, said you were one of the smartest people she'd ever met. She also said that you were incorruptible."

Winslaw must have been closer to her than Kylie had thought.

"I'm sorry. For Bernice. And for you. You could have made a difference in the world. A good difference."

"Oh, I'm going to make a difference, all right. You'll be hearing about it for years to come."

Playfully, he tapped his temple as though to remind himself of something. "Oh, that's right. You won't be around. What a shame."

She rolled her eyes. "Are you going to murder me just like you did Bernice and McCrane?"

He laughed. "You've got spunk. I'll give you that. Too bad it's not going to save you. Pretty soon, I'll have enough money to give me the power to turn this country around and take it back to what it used to be. The governor is stepping down. People will look to me for leadership."

"You're sick."

He backhanded her.

Her face throbbed, and she did her best to ignore it. When she was able to speak again, she said, "You won't win. People will see you for what you are and be disgusted by it. The trouble with people like you is that they become so good at lying, they start to believe their own lies."

He looked like he wanted to hit her again. "You don't know what you're talking about. The people will rise up and need a leader. A strong leader who will pull them out of the mess that our country is in." His voice grew with every word until he was shouting, but he seemed unaware of it.

"It will be me that they turn to. *Me.* Do you understand?" Spittle gathered at the corners of his mouth. At the same time, his face turned more and more florid, and she wondered if he was having a stroke. She remained quiet as he pulled into the parking lot at the factory.

He stopped the car and pulled her from it. After marching her into the building, he tied her to a chair with a length of rope. Immediately, she noted that the machinery and supplies had been removed. Obviously, Winslaw had been planning this.

"I hated to get rid of everything, but the insurance settlement will come in handy. I'll start over. Bigger and better."

Insurance? "What are you going to do?"

"You'll see."

With that, he strode away from her toward the exit, pouring a can of gasoline over the floor as he went.

"You're going to torch your own factory?" Terror raced through her at the idea of being trapped inside the building as it went up in flames.

"Thanks to you and your boyfriend, it's been compromised. Good thing it's insured. I'll end up with a boatload of cash and be able to set up operations somewhere else."

"You try collecting on the insurance money, and they'll know it was you." She had to keep him talking.

"I made a point of reporting vagrants holing up in the factory, setting fires to keep warm. As for you, it isn't much of a stretch to think that you returned to snoop around some more."

"Nobody's going to believe this was an accident. The police will see the ropes and the chair."

"You know as well as I do that the ropes and chair will be burned in the fire. I won't say it's been nice knowing you. So cliché. I have some other loose ends to tie up, so you'll forgive me if I take off."

With that, he struck a match then dropped it before he exited the building. The gas he'd poured on the floor ignited immediately.

Even knowing it was hopeless, Kylie fought against the cruel bite of the rope. Fear washed through her as the heat of the flames grew stronger. The idea of being burned alive gave new energy to her struggles against the rope, but nothing was going to break it. With the acceptance that she was going to die, regret settled in her heart. She wished she had told Josh that she loved him, that she had never stopped loving him. It was too late for that; just as she feared it was too late for her.

A prayer tumbled from her lips.

It didn't seem strange to be praying. Sometime in the nightmare of staying alive in the mountains, her faith had returned. How had she ever gotten along without it?

She was grateful she'd made her peace with the

Lord. She'd spent so much time being angry with Him, even when she'd known better and had actively rejected Him and His teachings in the last year. But beneath it all, the belief that had sustained her through so much of her life was still alive. Still breathing.

"Forgive me, Lord, for having been so stubborn. You did everything You could to help me see the truth, and I was too foolish to look. Whatever happens, I know You love me."

Smoke began to fill the room. She prayed it would take her before the flames, flames that were even now eating their way through the room. It was only a matter of minutes before they reached her.

Josh smelled the smoke as soon as he arrived at the factory. He'd been right. Winslaw had brought her here. He punched in 911, gave a terse description, then hung up. There was no time.

Fear such as he'd never known sent a frenzied path down his spine at the idea of Kylie burning alive. He had to get to her. Every prayer he'd ever uttered raced through his mind as he pled for Kylie's life.

"Please, Lord, keep her safe until I can get to her."

He pushed open the door, an acrid odor filling the air. He shielded his eyes and nose the best he could. The old building was going up with alarming speed.

Within him, an angry beast stirred and stretched out the claws of a predator. He'd protect her. No matter what. Even if it meant sacrificing his own life to do so. He loved her.

Had he waited too long to tell her? *Lord, please watch over Kylie until I can get to her.* Had the Lord heard his prayer? He didn't know.

The warehouse was huge. How did he go about finding her? "Kylie? Kylie! Where are you?"

Flames jumped from place to place, playing hopscotch. When one passageway was blocked, he turned to another, only to find it blocked, as well. He stayed low, all the while shouting her name. Smoke hoarsened his voice, reducing it to a grunt, but he refused to quit.

Something caught his attention, a sound different from the crackle of the flames. He paused, listened. Had he imagined it? No.

A faint voice reached him. "Josh? Stay back."

"Kylie!"

"Go back. I'm surrounded by flames."

"Not happening." He followed her voice, fighting his way through the conflagration, and then saw her bound to the chair. He stopped, struggling to breathe and to absorb the terrifying scene.

"Hold on," he shouted over the crack of fire and the hiss of smoke. "I'm coming."

Getting to Kylie meant walking through fire. He would have done that and more if it meant saving the life of the woman he loved. His heart stopped at the sight of her, helpless and afraid. Panic flared in her eyes while her mouth trembled as the fire drew ever closer.

Winslaw would pay for this. He would pay dearly.

The grim promise fueling his determination, Josh fought the ropes that bound her, even as a flame singed his arm. Seeing that he was getting nowhere with the knots, he kicked the chair legs, breaking them, then lifted her into his arms, despite her hands and legs still tied to the chair. His injured leg buckled for a moment, and he wasted valuable seconds straightening it.

Now he had to reverse his steps, this time carrying her. He hunched over and did his best to shield her from the worst of the blaze.

If ever he needed the Lord's protection, it was now. A prayer on his lips, he forged ahead. "Hang on," he shouted and ran through the wall of fire.

It took only seconds to make it to the other side of the blaze, but those seconds were the longest of his life. He ignored the intensity of the heat. He ignored the hiss of the smoke. He ignored the roar of the flames.

He ignored everything but saving Kylie.

Sparks landed on his arm, igniting the sleeve of his jacket. With both arms around Kylie, he wasn't able to put out the flames and did his best to protect her from them. Pain speared through him, but he scarcely noticed.

Outside, he carried her away from the factory and lowered her to the ground. After putting out the flames on his sleeve, he ran his hands over her. Nothing appeared to be broken. When she got to her feet, he steadied her as she swayed. "Are you okay?" he asked.

"Never mind about me. Your arm." Her eyes filled with tears.

"It'll heal." He brushed his lips over hers. "I thought I'd lost you. I thought I'd lost you." His voice broke.

She wasn't given the opportunity to respond when the scream of sirens screeched through the frigid air.

"The EMTs are here," he said and was glad to note that his voice had steadied.

They were both checked out and treated for smoke inhalation. The burn on his arm was wrapped in gauze.

It wasn't the first time he'd endured burns. While deployed in the Stand, he'd pulled a buddy out of a burning building, his hands and arms suffering second-and third-degree burns. The burns had healed, though he still bore the scars. These wounds would heal, as well.

"Are you sure you don't want to go to the hospital?" Kylie asked.

"I'll be fine." He was a lot more interested in finding Winslaw than he was in seeing a doctor. "Do you know where Winslaw went?"

"He said something about tying up a loose end."

Loose end? Kyllensgaard and McCrane were dead. Who did that leave? And then it came to him. The LG's grandfather. The change of will. He had to do it today or it would be too late.

Josh grabbed her arm and urged her to the truck.

"Where are we going?" she asked.

"To prevent another murder."

They found Winslaw in his grandfather's room, his hands gripping a pillow, holding it over the elderly man's face. Redken appeared to be asleep.

"It's over, Winslaw," Josh said. "You're done."

Surprise flickered in his eyes before he said, "You've got nothing on me."

"Really?" Josh motioned Kylie in so that Winslaw could see her.

"Why won't you die?" he shouted in furious disbelief upon seeing her. In the same instant, he pulled a gun from his waistband.

Before Josh could react, help came from an

unexpected source. Redken sliced a hand across Winslaw's wrist, causing him to drop the gun.

Kylie snatched up the gun and pointed it at the lieutenant governor.

"You made war on a woman?" his grandfather wheezed. "Have I taught you nothing? And then you try to kill me? I should have known it was only my money you were interested in."

Kylie stared Winslaw down. "Now it's your turn to be afraid."

SEVENTEEN

It was time. Time to tell Josh of her feelings for him, feelings that had only intensified over the last hour after he'd saved her from the fire.

They could have both died in the warehouse inferno, and she refused to allow another minute to go by without telling him that she loved him. Life was too fragile to waste time wondering what might have been.

But she wasn't given the opportunity.

She had the satisfaction of seeing Winslaw being led away in cuffs, protesting at the top of his voice, and then she and Josh were whisked away to make statements to the authorities where they were split up to give testimony. The feds, in the form of the ATF, were brought in and statements had to be made all over again. The Alcohol, Tobacco, Firearms and Explosives people grilled them until Kylie was falling-down tired.

"Tell us why you didn't go to the authorities when you first found out about McCrane and Winslaw," an agent directed.

"As I said *earlier*," she said with heavy emphasis, "we didn't have any proof. Think about it. Would you have believed us if we'd gone to you with a picture of the two men together and nothing else?"

The agent had the grace to blush. "Probably not."

The questions continued until both the local police and federal agency were satisfied. Exhausted, she and Josh stumbled out of the precinct. She needed a shower in the worst way followed by sleep.

"Shall I take you home?" he asked.

She shook her head. "Let's go back to the safe house."

Though she could have gone to her condo, she couldn't stomach the idea of facing the mess she would encounter there. But that wasn't the real reason she suggested they return to the safe house. She wanted more time with Josh. The future was by no means settled.

The following morning, they packed up their belongings. She looked about the S&J safe house and found herself reluctant to leave. Though they'd been there for only a short while, it had felt like home in a way her condo never had. Because she had shared it with Josh. A little hum danced in her throat at the thought.

"What now?" Josh asked.

"I have a story to write." She paused. "And you?"

"I need to go back to work. My vacation is over."

"Some vacation." How did she thank him for what he'd done for her? Would he be insulted if she offered to pay him?

"Thank you. You saved my life."

He nodded. "I think we're pretty well even given that you saved my life, too."

She wanted to say so much more that her jaw ached from keeping it inside. Did she have the courage to tell him what was in her heart? The moment was snatched from her when his phone rang.

His gaze never leaving hers, he answered the call. "Gideon. Yeah, I was just heading into work now. I'll be there in forty-five minutes." He closed the phone. "My boss."

"Oh." She was hoping they'd have more time before they had to return to their lives. More time to find out the answer to the question *Who might we become together?* "I guess you'd better go."

"I'll see you home first."

Whatever she'd been about to say would keep. The ride to his place, where she would pick up her car, was quiet, each wrapped up in their own thoughts.

"I'll see you later," Josh said upon letting her out.

"Later."

She didn't want to leave him with things left unsaid between them. Reluctantly, she got out of the car and went into her condo. She had to set about getting her life back on track. The mindless chores of cleaning the condo and doing laundry gave her time to think. Perhaps she and Josh could have a future together.

A frisson of pleasure zinged through her at the thought.

By the time she had put the condo to rights and had outlined a story that would no doubt rock not just the state capital but the entire state and much of the Southwest, she was well and truly tired.

She reflected on all that had happened in the last days. With the photo and the prototype of the Glock switch as evidence, there was even more proof of what McCrane and Winslaw had been up to.

So when she went to bed it was with the expectation of sleeping soundly. And she did, until her dreams took her back to the prison camp, then inexplicably placed her in the burning building. Cries from mothers and children segued into the crackle and hiss of fire and smoke.

"No! No!"

She reached for a weapon, anything with which to defend herself. Grasping wildly, she grabbed the first thing her hand encountered.

A scream awakened her. She looked about to see where it had come from, only to realize that it was her own. Disoriented, drenched in sweat, she sat up in bed and found herself gripping a lamp, ready to wield it like a weapon.

She remained sitting, shaking uncontrollably. When the worst of it was over, she tried standing. Her knees buckled, but she stiffened them and took a step. The act of forcing one foot in front of the other took her back to the time in the mountains when she had struggled dragging the travois. She had gotten through that; she would get through this, as well.

She'd learned from experience that there was no point in trying to go back to sleep and went through a ritual she'd developed. First prayer. Ever since she'd invited the Lord back into her life, she'd made prayer a priority.

Hot chocolate, because even though she was covered in sweat, she also had the chills. A warm shower, to wash away the sweat. The familiar routine calmed, soothed. And, finally, work.

She needed the work, the doing. She booted up her laptop and worked on an article, all the while doing her best to put this latest episode out of her mind, but it wouldn't stay in the tidy box where she assigned it. It snuck back, creeping into her thoughts in such an insidious manner that she finally let it have its way.

Deal with it now. Get it over with. She wrapped her arms around herself and rocked back and forth. When the tears came, she let them have their way.

Why now? Everything was going well. What if it rendered her unable to write as it had in previous instances when she'd fallen behind in meeting her deadlines?

But that wasn't the worst of it.

There'd be no future with Josh. There'd be no future with anyone.

Josh knew there were things left unsaid between him and Kylie. He'd longed to tell her of his feelings, but Gideon's call had postponed that. Maybe it was just as well. They both needed a little normalcy before they delved into whatever there was between them.

The assignment he'd been given was a one-day protection detail, escorting a teenage media star to her hotel, followed by shopping and then a luncheon being held in her honor, all the while shielding her from the paparazzi. Her regular bodyguard, who would normally have been on the job, had suffered a brief bout of food poisoning and had been in the hospital overnight. By midnight, he was back on duty.

Josh had never been so relieved to end an assignment. Going shopping and attending luncheons weren't in his wheelhouse. He returned home and slept in his own bed for the first time in over a week. Not surprisingly, he slept soundly.

The following morning, he drove to Kylie's condo. Was it too soon to tell her of his feelings? Did she need more time? The last thing he wanted to do was frighten her by coming on too hard, too fast. She'd proved herself time and again in the mountains and afterward, but he knew that she still didn't believe in herself as he did.

He rang the doorbell, waited impatiently.

Worry danced through him the moment he saw her face. It looked ravaged, as though she'd been seriously sick. What had happened?

And then he knew. A PTSD episode. The signs were all there. The skin drawn tautly over her cheekbones. The shaking hands. The smile that wasn't a smile at all.

He reached for her, but she neatly sidestepped his embrace. He followed her inside.

"You had another episode." It wasn't a guess but a statement of fact.

She nodded.

"Let me help you. You don't have to do it alone."

"I can handle it. Go now, please." She held the door open, clearly indicating that he should leave.

He ignored that and closed the door behind him. "Can you tell me about it?"

She took a seat on the sofa and, with a heavy air of resignation, gave the gist of the attack.

He nodded, absorbing what she said, all the while wondering how he could help her defeat the terrors that had taken hold of her.

"You don't have to be alone." Had he already said that? "I'll stay. We'll deal with it together. Just like we did in the mountains."

She shook her head even as he said the words. "I do better on my own. I have a routine. Besides, you have work."

He sliced through the air to dismiss the idea that he'd put work before her. No job was more important than Kylie.

Tears ran in tiny rivulets down her cheeks. He longed to wipe them away but didn't dare.

"I can't be with you, Josh. If you're honest with yourself, you'll see that I'm right and that it won't work. I'm too broken."

It tore his heart into slivers of pain to hear the words. "You shouldn't be alone." And he realized his error immediately.

Her head came up. "Who are you to tell me what I should or shouldn't do?"

"I'm sorry. That came out wrong."

"Go. Please, just go."

It wasn't in his nature to give up. He wanted to rail against the trauma that had her in its grip. He could fight that, but he couldn't fight her.

This wasn't over. He'd make her see that they belonged together. But it wouldn't be today.

Kylie sat back, startled when she noted that she'd been working for five hours straight. Satisfied with her work, she saved it, then turned off the computer.

In the last week, Winslaw had been arrested for murder, conspiracy to commit murder, weapons trafficking and a host of other felonies. In addition, he was facing RICO charges. If he was convicted, the Racketeer Influenced and Corrupt Organizations charges alone would keep him in prison for decades. That, plus the murder charges, would see to it that he didn't see the outside of a prison for the rest of his life.

It seemed like an eternity since she'd seen Josh. A dozen times, she'd been tempted to go to him, to tell him that she loved him with all of her heart and always would. And a dozen times, she'd rejected the impulse.

She was broken. Her experiences in the prison camp had irrevocably damaged her. How did she tell him that she couldn't let anyone, not even him, get close to her?

She'd once thought she was strong, but that belief had been shattered by the PTSD, which had her questioning everything she'd once believed about herself. She'd pushed herself to finish three articles in record time, afraid if she slowed down even slightly, the PTSD would lay claim to her again. She'd shop them around to various news magazines and pray they'd be picked up.

A tiny movement caught her attention as a spider wove a small web in the corner of the kitchen.

She watched the progress, noting how the creature took its time. It didn't push itself. No, it simply kept at the task, patient and meticulous.

Her therapist had tasked her to be aware of occasions when she was impatient with herself and to find new and more healthy ways of dealing with life's challenges. When the doorbell rang, she looked at her sweats and wished she'd taken time earlier to change her clothes and brush her hair out from its straggly ponytail.

Josh stood there, tall, strong and unswerving. He was everything she'd ever wanted. "Can I come in?"

She stepped back, gestured him inside.

"I couldn't stay away any longer," he said and drew her to him.

Awareness spiked when he skimmed her cheek with the back of his hand.

She couldn't pull away, especially not when his voice turned soft and his touch was as gentle as thistledown.

"You told me once you were a survivor. You survived the prison camp. You survived being chased by killers in the mountains. You survived the fire. Are you telling me now that you're going to let one puny episode of PTSD defeat you?"

She pulled back. Puny? Is that what he thought? "You don't know anything about it."

"Then tell me."

"If you'd been with me during that episode, I

could have hurt you, knocked you unconscious. Maybe worse." She shuddered, thinking of what could have happened.

"I've done my own share of surviving. I was out in those mountains with you, if you remember." He slanted her a look inexplicably filled with humor. "Do you think someone who weighs a buck five is going to take me out?"

The question was asked lightly, but she heard the challenge in the words.

Josh was that rare combination, a man both strong and vulnerable, hard when needed but tender in the right places. Right now, it was the vulnerable and tender parts that called to her in ways she was only beginning to understand. Eleven years ago, she'd been a young girl, more in love with the idea of being in love than she was with a man. Today, she was a woman who recognized the difference.

Impulsively, she pressed her cheek to his, the barest caress.

He held her in place when she started to pull away. "Stay," he said, his voice so filled with pleading and hope that she was nearly brought to tears. "Just stay."

The knowledge that he was as moved as she was strengthened her. It also scared her.

She wanted a future with him, a home, a family. Could she handle that, knowing a PTSD episode could launch a sneak attack at any moment?

"Leaving you was the hardest thing I ever did," he said. "I never forgot you, never stopped loving you."

"Nor I you."

"I love you. I always have. I always will." With infinite gentleness, he kissed her, a kiss filled with sweet promise.

She didn't resist and returned the kiss. "And I love you. You fill me up. You make me want more. To *be* more."

"You are everything I've ever wanted," he said. "I don't deserve you, but I'll do my best to be the man you deserve." She heard it in his voice, the fierceness and the love.

Frissons of warmth raced down her spine. "We have the next fifty or sixty years to work on it."

"You're pretty smart for a lady in sweats and a ponytail."

There would be a tomorrow for them. And all the tomorrows after that. She was exactly where she wanted to be.

Forever.

* * * * *